The Gods of Fate – Book III

Hindsight

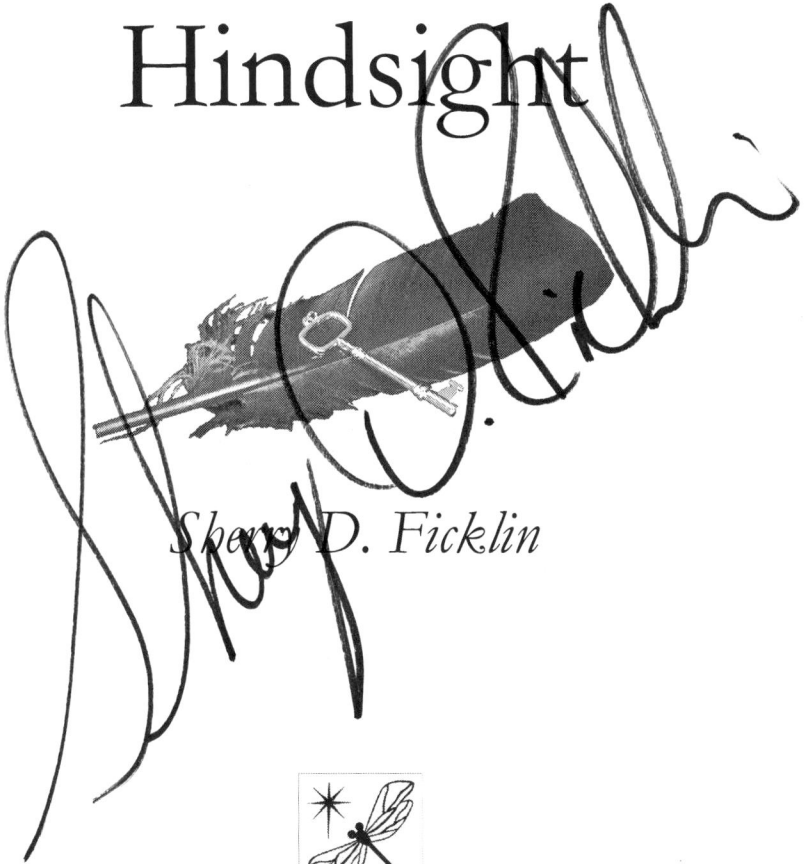

Sherry D. Ficklin

Young Adult Fantasy from
Dragonfly Publishing, Inc.

Hindsight

The Gods of Fate – Book III
Young Adult Fantasy

Paperback Edition
EAN 978-1-936381-38-8
ISBN 1-936381-38-9

Story Text Copyright ©2011 Sherry D. Ficklin
Cover Art Copyright ©2011 Dragonfly Publishing, Inc.
Dragonfly Logo Copyright ©2001 Terri L. Branson

Published in the United States of America by
Dragonfly Publishing, Inc.
Website: www.dragonflypubs.com

Gods of Fate Series:

FORESIGHT
(Book I)

SECOND SIGHT
(Book II)

HINDSIGHT
(Book III)

Acknowledgements

Writing this series has been an amazing journey for me.

I want to first thank the wonderful people who made it all possible, Terri, Pat, and Janet, my team over at Dragonfly Publishing. Thank you so much for taking a chance on me and my books. You will never know how much you ladies mean to me.

I would also like to thank the readers who have followed Grace through the books. Without you guys my words would never have had wings.

As always, I need to thank my amazing family and friends for all their love and support. You make me feel blessed and humbled every day.

Special thanks to my extremely talented sister-in-law Monica who gave my characters faces and to the beautiful Rebecca S. who is the best alpha-reader and friend a girl could ask for.

And finally, to my husband whose patience and support knows no boundaries. I couldn't have done it without you!

Thank you! ~ Sherry

OLYMPIANS:

Apollo [Sun God]
Calliope [One of the Muses]
Chance [Demi-God]
Charron [Ferryman of the Dead]
Eris [Goddess of Discord]
Eros [God of Lust]
Grace [the Harbinger]
Hades [God of the Underworld]
Hephaestus [God of the Forge]
Hermes [Messenger God]
Mnemosyne [Goddess of Memory]
Pan [God of the Wild]
Pandora [Keeper of the Urn]
Persephone [Queen of the Underworld]
Prometheus [God of Foresight]
Psyche [Demi-Goddess]
Sybil [Demi-Goddess]

FAE:

Christopher [Seelie Sidhe]
Phoenix [Seelie Sidhe]
Lorna [Seelie Sidhe]
Luna [Seelie Sidhe]
Lynx [Unseelie Sidhe]
Lucinda [Seelie Sidhe]
Phillip [Seelie Sidhe]
Ghared [Seelie Sidhe]
Mimble [Demi-Fae]

GUARDIANS:

Baal [Mehmet the Second]
James [Alexander the Great]
Michael [Charlemagne]
Samael [Gaius Julius Caesar]

For my mom.

Everything I ever learned about love and loyalty I learned from you.

PROLOGUE

CHRIS was still fuming when he arrived back in the main square of Aletheia, the capitol city of the Fae.

His chest rose and fell, heavy from the run back from the waterfall and from the sting of Grace's rejection. Pausing to wipe his hair from his eyes, he looked up at the glittering dome of The Hall of Memory.

He had watched Grace for some time now, trying to figure out a way to get closer to her, a way past the walls she kept around herself. In all his years, he had never met anyone like her. Grace Archer was a goddess. A real one. Daughter of the demi-goddess Pandora and the Titan Prometheus, Grace was an actual living, breathing Olympian.

She was strong, but at the same time fragile. Each time he touched her, he feared she might slip away like sand between his fingers. When he was with her, it was as if the stars had aligned. Being away from her made him anxious and irritable.

He jogged up the steps to the open doors of the hall and silently cursed the Guardian James for interfering yet again.

Today he had been so close to making a connection with her that he could almost taste it. But the beautiful, mysterious, and infuriating Grace had once again held Chris at arm's length. It was not James' fault, although it was tempting to lay blame there. Each time Chris saw James with Grace, jealousy gagged him like a bitter fruit. Something about James made Grace pull away. If Chris could only get her alone for just a few minutes, he was sure he could break through her defenses. That was why he had decided to confront her in the Hall of Memory.

Chris paced the marble floor, walking slowly along the edges of the massive mosaic sun set in the floor.

There was mutual attraction. He could feel that much. But there was also something else, a deep tug in the back of his mind that made it impossible to think about anything else. Something sat uncomfortably on the hazy edges of his vision, demanding that he go to her. It was a need he could not deny. He had never felt so much for anyone. Though they had only known each other a short while, he recognized exactly what it was.

It was madness. It was frustration. It was love.

And he would do whatever it took to make her see that.

Near the shadowy wall, Chris paced back and forth, as if he could bring her to him with nothing but sheer desire.

He heard someone climb the steps.

Grace entered the Hall. Wearing a red leather fighting outfit, her chin was held high and a fierce look of determination was etched on her face. Sunlight cast a fiery halo around her red hair and her eyes shone emerald green.

Realizing that she hadn't noticed him lurking in the shadows, he opened his mouth to announce himself. But quickly snapped his jaws shut. In a combination of curiosity and blatant obsession, he stepped behind a large urn and crouched out of sight, pulling his Fae wings close to his body.

Why had she come here? And why had James been so much against it?

Chris had overheard them arguing near the waterfall. He had only listened to reassure himself that there were no romantic ties between them. Hearing Grace reject the Guardian had filled his heart with a joy he had never known.

James loved Grace. That much was no surprise. But Grace didn't love James.

When Grace said she was coming to the Hall of Memory, Chris knew it would be his chance, possibly his last chance, to convince her that *he* was her true love.

Now he hid in the shadows like some pathetic stalker. He shook his head in shame. But something held him there, silent, as Grace pulled the doors closed behind her and moved to the center of the room.

"Hello, Grace." The soft female voice of the Hall of Memory echoed in the chamber. "What would you like to see today?"

"I'd like to see the Beltane festival," Grace requested. "Just one more time."

She stepped back until her shoulders were flat against the far wall and watched, transfixed, as a heavy fog filled the center of the chamber.

Slowly, a vision appeared in the fog like a movie being projected onto a cloud.

Chris was staggered by the images in front of him. In the fog image, he danced with Grace and kissed her. She looked so happy. For that matter, so did he.

Shock was quickly replaced by confusion. When had all this happened? He remembered the Beltane Festival. He danced with a few friends, drank too much mead cider, and returned alone to his room. He hadn't even known Grace back then.

Why would the Hall show memories of them together? Was it some kind of bizarre fantasy Grace had created? He shook his head, dismissing that idea. No, the Hall of Memory showed only the truth, history as it actually happened. There was no way to manipulate the images to show false histories. His mind flashed from one possibility to another at the speed of light, but nothing made any sense.

Chris started to stand, but froze when he looked back at Grace. She sat on the floor with her back against the wall and her knees pulled to her chest, cradling herself as tears rolled down her face. She smiled through the silent sobs wracking her body and wiped her eyes with her sleeve.

He flashed to an image of her looking like that, tears pouring from her eyes but in another place. A dark place. She was being restrained by James, who held her arms behind her back as she sobbed and fought to free herself.

The half-formed memory slipped from his mind, as the scene in the fog changed. Now they were together in Grace's room, entwined on the bed. Chris watched Grace snuggle against his chest. Her breathing slowed and she fell asleep in his arms. In the vision Chris stroked her face before closing his eyes.

Then memory fog evaporated into nothing.

Grace wiped her eyes one more time. "Thank you," she whispered.

She struggled to her feet and headed for the exit.

Too stunned to speak, Chris watched Grace pull open the doors.

She raised her face into the bright daylight, tilting her head up as if basking in the sun's warmth. Then she squared her shoulders and vanished.

Dazed, Chris stepped out from behind the urn and shook out his wings. He walked over and closed the heavy doors. Then he moved to the center of the chamber.

"Hello, Christopher," the disembodied voice said. "What would you like to see today?"

Chris didn't have to think about the question. "Show me everything."

CHAPTER 1

She blazes with battle fury out in front of her army,
a girl, a warrior queen. ~ Virgil

A gothic ebony throne exploded into dust and rubble at Grace's bare feet.

With an approving nod, her father Prometheus waved his hand and cleared the mess into oblivion. The Temple of the All Gods now sat empty, only the sound of Grace's satisfied clap echoing in the round chamber.

"That's the last one," Prometheus said, patting his daughter on the back. The Titan stood bare-chested with a braid of black hair trailing down the center of his back between long white wings. Thick pink scars crisscrossed his tanned chest, a visual reminder of his time in Tartarus.

It had been a long couple of weeks, or however much time passed in the real world, since Grace had returned to Olympus. Time passed much differently on Olympus than in the human world. It was like comparing dog years to human years, and Grace didn't really pay much attention to the days as they ticked by. Instead she kept herself busy doing anything she could, to distract from the memories of the people she left behind.

Grace and her father had taken up the task of cleaning and restoring the ruined temples and statues. The effort was not a small one, even for a demi-goddess and a Titan.

"What now?" Grace asked, wiping her long sleeve on a small bronze amphora to clear away caked dust.

"What do you think?" he asked, motioning to the empty space.

Grace was exhausted. The Gods didn't actually sleep, but that part of her genetic chemistry hadn't fully kicked in yet. She still slept like the dead almost every night. After a day of training or cleaning or building, she would return to her room and crash. She still could not bring herself to think of it as a temple. Rallying against the weariness that had set deep into her bones, she focused.

"Well, where are the demi-god temples?" she asked.

They focused their efforts on the temples along the main path through Olympus, the one that lead to the main temple, the Temple of All the Gods. Few of the Greek Gods remained on Olympus. Many had surrendered their immortality and moved on, others had been destroyed, but some had made their homes in the human world. Hermes, for example, still retained a temple on Olympus' plane of existence, though he preferred to spend his days in a humble beach house on the coast of Cape Hatteras where he could continue his search for the perfect wave and the perfect hotdog. Hermes was not only a good friend, but his occasional poker night invitations were a welcome distraction.

"The demi-gods have no temples on Olympus," Prometheus answered while examining a blank bit of wall. "If they are here, they mostly stay inside their parent's temples. It's the same reason there were only twelve thrones. Only the Gods are allowed inside the Temple of the Gods, or so it was in the days before the Dissension."

He tilted his head back and forth for a minute before producing a golden ball of energy in his large hand, flinging it at the wall. A hole blasted through the marble in a perfect circle, creating a window from where a beam of shimmering light shown into the chamber, directly in the center of the room.

The Dissension was the final fall of the Olympians, when the Mother Goddess herself had reprimanded the Gods. She had been angry over the way they treated the humans and the Fae, so she laid down the law. As a matter of fact, she had done it twice.

It occurred to Grace that no matter where she went, on Earth, in Faerie, even on Olympus, there always seemed to be some type of segregation. Phoenix and Lynx, the Queen's guard and Phoenix's true love, were forbidden to be together because he was Unseelie and she was Seelie Sidhe. It was unfair, unjust, and it raked Grace's nerves. The same self-important nonsense kept the half-gods and demi-gods separate and beneath the Olympian Gods. The acceptance of Grace came more easily because of her father being a Titan and her mother, Pandora, being a demi-goddess, making Grace more than a half-goddess. Plus the fact that while the other Olympians' powers were diminished, hers were growing stronger. Grace had a 'no questions asked' place among the remaining Gods.

"The first thing we should do is change that," she said decisively. "Maybe Hermes can get a list of all the remaining half-gods and demi-gods. We can build temples for them and do some re-arranging in the main temple. I mean, there's so few of you left, it seems stupid not to include everyone."

"We, dear daughter." Prometheus slid a muscular arm across Grace's shoulders. "There are so few of us left. And, you are absolutely right. It is time to unify our family. I believe the time has come to join together and unite in a new purpose. So many immortals are wandering aimlessly through eternity. It saddens me to see it. Perhaps you could change all that."

"What can I do?" Grace asked.

Grace had only recently discovered her Olympian heritage. Her mother had fled the pantheon upon discovering she was pregnant, and Grace was raised with no knowledge of their existence. At least, not until a crazed demi-goddess had attacked Grace at her high school graduation.

That was less than a year ago, but to Grace it felt like another lifetime.

Even after discovering the truth, Grace chose to live in the Fae city of Aletheia with her aunt Phoenix.

A memory of the real reason she decided to stay in faerie swam to the front of her mind.

Chris.

She gasped at the sudden sharp pain in her chest. It hit her every time she thought of him, like ripping the bandage off a wound that hadn't yet healed. The pain was sharp, immediate, and always seemed to catch her off guard. Part of her wanted to get lost in the memory, to wrap herself in it and roll around as the pain ate at her.

No, she told herself. Pushing away the memory and the pain, she pulled back her shoulders and held up her head.

Prometheus dropped a hand her shoulder and turned her to face him.

"Grace, you have the loyalty of some of the most powerful beings in existence. You have more powers than the rest of us combined. You have proven yourself courageous and honest. I believe you can give them purpose once again."

Grace let that roll around in her head for a moment. It must be a dull existence, just hanging out on Olympus or wherever and doing nothing. Maybe they needed something to do, like a cause. Maybe, like the Guardians, they could use their limited powers to protect mankind.

Prometheus patted her arms and then released her. "You have a lesson, I believe. You should go. Apollo does not like to be kept waiting."

Without warning, Apollo appeared.

Unlike Prometheus, Apollo had no wings. His bare chest, however, was sculpted in muscular perfection and his flawless skin held a golden glow.

With a curt nod Prometheus vanished, leaving Grace to her grumpy teacher.

Apollo agreed, at Prometheus' request, to try to teach Grace the fundamental abilities of a Goddess.

They assured that her visions, her healing, and her ability to teleport were just the tip of the iceberg. The idea of gaining any new abilities made Grace nauseous. The ones she had were enough trouble. Power, she came to realize, always carried a price. Like everything else in life, the price was almost too much to ask, at the very limits of what you could tolerate and survive. Her whole existence felt that way now. As if she was walking the knife-edge between what she could survive, and what would send her spiraling into oblivion.

The problem with Apollo was that his incredible vanity was damaged by the fact that Grace didn't, nor had she ever, found him overwhelmingly attractive. He was, in every conceivable way, the golden boy of Olympus. His face was long, but not too long, and was framed by a head of sunshine yellow curls that made his bright blue eyes stand out like lightning in the darkness. His jaw was square and, as Grace once observed, his nose leaned slightly to the left. Most people never noticed the tiny flaw, because he spent so much of his power making himself irresistible. He was accustomed to women falling all over themselves to get close to him. Grace just saw him as a specimen in a jar, something to be studied from a safe distance. Yes, he had given her the silver bow of Artemis that had allowed her to defeat Lilith. But she also had seen his wrath firsthand in a curse he had laid upon a young Oracle who, with great nerve, had refused his advances.

In short, Grace thought Apollo was a narcissist. The Goddess only knew what he thought of her.

"Now, are we ready to begin?" he asked with his hands clenched at his sides.

Grace nodded and twisted her long red hair into a bun at the back of her neck. She wore a flowing Grecian gown that hung from her shoulders in perfect folds and cinched at her waist by golden cords. It was green, like her eyes, and more comfortable than it looked. It was a gift from Eros who convinced her that to assume the role of a goddess meant dressing the part. Reluctantly, she traded the corset tops and leather pants she wore in Faerie for the more regal dress. It never wrinkled, nor did it tear or get dirty, no matter what she did in it. It was as light as air and as soft as silk. Basically, she loved it.

"Let's do it," Grace said as she manifested her silver bow into her hands.

With a smooth motion, she notched the wooden practice arrow. Apollo had given these to her the last time after she almost accidentally shot him with one of the extremely lethal silver arrows she used in battle. Taking a deep breath to center herself, she aimed for Apollo.

Wrinkling his nose, he placed a single finger on the point of the arrow and moved aside the bow. "Not archery practice today. I'm going to teach you how to fight with energy bursts as the Gods do." He folded his arms across his chest, waiting for her to challenge him.

When the Gods fought, they had the ability to throw balls of electricity at each other. They manifested in all colors, and Grace knew from being hit by a few, they packed a serious punch. However, they were not lethal, unlike the silver arrows Apollo gave her on her eighteenth birthday. It was strictly forbidden for the Gods to kill each other. Maim, sure. Zap, absolutely. But killing another god was a one-way ticket to Tartarus, the eternal torture chamber of the Underworld.

In the past, she was hesitant to lean this particular ability, mostly because people continuously told her she must tap into her inner anger to do it. Since becoming immortal, she carried this darkness inside her, a seething rage she could barely restrain. It frightened her. And so she refused. Adamantly. Until today.

"Okay, let's give it a shot," she said, lowering the bow and sending it back to her temple with the blink of an eye.

Apollo crossed the chamber from her and dropped into a defensive crouch. He said nothing as his eyes shimmered red and then turned back to blue. If he was surprised by her response, he didn't show it.

Grace offered a curt nod and mimicked his posture.

Slowly, the two began to circle the room.

With a flick of his wrist, a glowing ball appeared in Apollo's hand.

Grace flicked her wrist in the same gesture.

Nothing.

"You've held a burst before, have you not?" he asked, straightening out of the crouch, still holding the energy burst in the palm of his hand.

"Only once," she admitted. "Samael threw it at me and I caught it."

"You have to try to remember what it felt like," Apollo instructed. "Try to recall the feel of it in your hand."

Grace closed her eyes, trying to focus on the sensation. After a minute she shook her head. "I can't. It feels like forever ago, and I was so out of control when it happened."

Apollo smirked and without warning tossed the burst at her.

With a gasp, Grace dove to the ground.

He laughed. "Come on, you can do better than that." He created another burst in his hand and chucked it toward where Grace lay on the floor.

She rolled and it narrowly missed her, leaving a dark singe mark where she had been seconds earlier. "Hey, I just cleaned that."

Jumping to her feet she growled, reaching down into the dark pit inside herself that contained her rage. It bubbled up to the surface, bringing with it a ferocious snarl. She felt it slide over her skin like oil, thick and cold.

This time when Apollo attacked, Grace was ready for him. He threw the burst and she reached forward, plucking it out of the air with so much speed that the movement was a blur. She drew up instinctively to throw it back at Apollo.

He held out his hands. "Now, Grace, just concentrate on the feel of it."

She blinked and forced the anger back down, tightly locking the lid on it. The energy was warm in her hands, just on the edge between pleasure and pain. It was like a miniature thunderstorm in the palm of her hand. The color was created by sparks being carried by tiny tornadoes swirling so quickly that it was a blur of white and yellow.

For the first time, Grace understood what made the Gods, what made her, different. This amazing energy in the palm of her hand reminded her that once upon a time the Gods contained the power to cause storms like this in real size. And they did. They shook the Earth and rained fire from the skies. It was no wonder they were worshipped and feared. For the first time, she realized their loss and how greatly they were reduced. In a blink the burst was gone, simply melting into her skin.

"That was amazing," she admitted, breathless.

"That is your heritage." Apollo crossed the distance between them, taking her hand in an unusual gesture of kindness. "You are capable of so many things. You haven't imagination enough to fathom them. Tides will rise at your behest, cities will tremble, and lightning will strike at your command. That is what it is to be a goddess. That is your power to claim."

"I don't deserve that kind of power," Grace whispered.

"It is not a matter of deserving," he scoffed. "There is only having and being strong enough to wield."

Grace pulled her hand free. "Maybe it should be a matter of deserving."

"And who would be the judge of whether one deserves?" he asked.

Grace thought about that for a minute. Turning she looked at the empty chamber around them. She didn't feel fit to judge anyone. But there must be someone who could. Someone the immortals trusted, respected.

"You look exhausted," Apollo said. "Why don't you go rest? We will train more later."

He stepped back and vanished, leaving Grace alone in the glowing torchlight.

In a flash she was back in her own room. Slipping out of her gown and into a simple white nightdress, she crawled into bed and was asleep before her head made it to the pillow.

CHAPTER 2

No living man can send me to the shades before my time; no man of woman born, coward or brave, can shun his destiny. ~ Homer

CHRIS stumbled out of the Hall of Memory.

He bolted down the ivory steps, rushing toward the palace and his sister, Queen Lorna.

Images of foreign emotions pulsed behind his eyelids. He needed answers. Had the Hall of Memory shown him the truth? Had he lived a life with Grace that he could not remember? How could that be? He thought back. His own memories were faded and gray, like staring at a photograph of the past without actually remembering having lived the scene.

No, he told himself. It was not possible. It must be a mistake.

The Fae Palace was bustling with people. It was again time for the Queen's election. Seelie Sidhe Lords and Ladies came from all over to act as both representatives from their respective boroughs and to nominate a new leader. Lorna's term had lasted the standard ten years. It was possible she might be re-elected as monarch. Knowing his sister, she would be ready to pass on the mantle and do something new. Some monarchs ruled for a hundred years. Some only one term. Lately, more the latter.

Pushing past an emissary from the Westland, Chris made his way into Lorna's private rooms. Lynx, her personal guard, stood watch at the door to her library.

Lynx offered a half-bow, but even that left him towering above Chris. Large even for an Unseelie Sidhe, Lynx stood an intimidating six-foot and ten-inches with a halberd strapped across his back, not that he needed the weapon. Like all Unseelie, he bore tattoos on his back instead of wings. Lynx and his family had served the regent with faithful and brutal efficiency for over a thousand years. Stepping to the side, his warm brown eyes alert,

Lynx allowed Chris to push open the heavy door.

"Lorna?" Chris called, closing the door behind him.

"Over here," Lorna replied in a singsong voice.

Following the sound, he wound his way through the dusty stacks until he found his sister sitting cross-legged on the floor, a massive volume of what looked to be elfin poetry on her lap.

She smiled up at him with vivid eyes, her pearl-white wings fluttering. A pearl crown, nestled in a halo of golden hair, slipped to the side just a fraction. "What can I do for my big brother today?"

"I need to ask you something." Caught in a quick tide of affection, Chris reached down and tugged the crown back to center of her head. "I was at the Hall of memory today."

Lorna closed the book with a quick snap. She stood, dusting off the back of her long golden dress. "Why were you in the Hall of Memory?" she asked sharply.

Chris narrowed his eyes. Since the time they were children, he could always tell when his sisters were up to something. "What do you know?" he demanded.

Turning her back to him, Lorna replaced the heavy volume on the shelf. When she looked at him again, her face was a careful mask.

"I don't know what you are talking about." She brushed past him in a rush of crinkling fabric.

He grabbed her by the arm, jerking her to a stop. "Don't lie to me Lorna."

She pulled herself free. Frown lines pulled around her mouth and eyes. "What do you think you know?"

"I saw Grace and me. We were together, as if I'd known her for years, since the day she was born. But I know I just met her a few months ago. I saw us fighting Lilith together, even though I know I wasn't there. I saw us dancing on the night of the Beltane Festival, but I don't remember any of it." He rubbed his face with both hands. "How is that possible?"

Lorna stared at him, her mouth a hard line. After a long moment, she motioned for him to follow her.

They moved through the tall bookshelves until they came

upon a short arched door. Lorna pushed it open, revealing a chamber beyond. The room was round with one massive stained glass window that filtered light into the room in rainbow shards. The only furniture was a dark wooden writing desk with a matching chair and an ottoman of golden velvet.

"This is my reflection room," Lorna explained. "It's where I come to find peace, solace, and to clear my mind."

Chris said nothing, taking a seat on the rigid chair.

Lorna sat gracefully across from him. Folding her hands in her lap, she looked up to the sky. "Hermes, please join us."

Chris resisted the urge to shake the information from his sister. She knew something and was keeping tight-lipped about it, which only infuriated him more.

A minute later Hermes appeared in the room with a faint pop. His usual Hawaiian shirt and shorts were replaced by a black form-fitting wetsuit that dripped water onto the floor around his bare feet.

"What is it Lorna?" Hermes asked with irritation, his shaggy sun-bleached hair hanging in wet tangles at his neck. "I was surfing off the coast of Africa. Amazing swells this time of year."

"Chris has been to the Hall of Memory," she said, as if it was an explanation.

"Oh," Hermes said in a tone that sounded like a cross between shock and fear.

His anger reaching its limit, Chris pushed off the chair and took the needed steps that brought him toe-to-toe with Hermes. "You two need to start explaining. Now!"

"Chris, please," Lorna implored. "We are forbidden to speak of this."

"If we do," Hermes explained, "you will be trapped in Faerie forever. If we give you this truth and you ever leave this realm, you will die."

Chris stepped back. "What are you talking about?"

"The choice is yours," Hermes stated, frustration evident in his tone. "You know the consequences now. But remember, once said it cannot be undone."

"Just tell me!" Chris demanded.

"Your memory was altered," Lorna explained in a low voice. "By Mnemosyne."

"Wait—What? Why?"

"Because, my friend, you didn't survive the battle with Lilith," Hermes explained. "Grace was somehow able to prevent your soul from crossing over. She revived you. When Hades found out, he came and claimed you."

Chris sat back down, letting Hermes' words sink in. The events he had witnessed in the Hall of Memory were real. It was *his* memory that was the lie. Emotions inside him warred for dominance. Relief, grief, anger, and dismay all ebbed and flowed in overlapping swells.

"Wait," Chris said. "Then how am I alive? And why is my memory gone?"

"Grace went to the Underworld to get you back," Lorna answered, a single tear rolling down her cheek. "She struck a bargain with Hades. Your life in exchange for your memories of her. He wanted it to be as if you had never met. It was her punishment, the price she had to pay for your freedom."

"I was there," Hermes offered in a gentle voice. "It was horrible, but Grace did it so you could come back here and be with your family. So you could have a life."

Chris sat in stunned silence. All those times Grace cringed from him. All the lies she told him. She said she lost someone she loved, but the truth was she was just feeling guilty for loving him so little that she could bargain his very memories away to the God of the Dead. How could she claim to love him when she took the choice away from him? He never would have chosen to live a lie. Grace must have known that.

"The only ones who remember what really happened are those of us who were present when the deal was struck," Hermes added. "Everyone else forgot. It wasn't just you. And we were forbidden to tell you the truth or the deal would be forfeit and you would be reclaimed by Hades."

"That's why you have to stay here now." Lorna's tears fell freely. "No Gods may enter Faerie without invitation. As long as you stay here, you're safe."

Chris clenched his fists. "So now I am a prisoner, as well."

He stood, pacing the floor. Raking his hand through his hair, he growled. Grace was hiding in Olympus. She abandoned him to his fate and ran away. Now he was trapped in Faerie. He could not even grab her by the arms and shake the truth out of her.

"What gave her the right? Who does she think she is, taking that away from me?"

"Chris, please," Lorna begged. "I just wanted you home. And it was very hard for Grace."

"Hard for Grace. Yes, I just bet it was hard for Grace. She lied to me for months. I thought—I thought she loved me."

"Grace does love you," Hermes snapped. "Make no mistake. It nearly destroyed her to lose you."

"Who else knew about this?" Chris asked.

"As we said, only those who were present when the bargain was struck remembered. Myself, Lorna, James—"

Chris cut him off with a wave of his hand. "James? James knew about this?"

Of course, James knew. It was a clever plan, the ultimate way to ensure his victory. James stole Grace from him, convinced her to trade away his love like a bargaining chip in one of the Gods' petty games. And the lies. For months she lied to his face about everything. How could he ever have fallen in love with her? Twice? It made his insides twist just to think about it. In the sea of rising emotions, a winner was becoming clear.

"I don't want to hear anymore. I need to be alone."

Chris turned to leave.

"Wait!" Lorna called. "Where are you going?"

He turned, giving her a curt nod. "To my room, your majesty, seeing as how I am now a prisoner there."

"You aren't a prisoner," Lorna countered. "Please, Chris. Don't shut me out."

"Lorna, you are my sister, my kin," Chris said. "And you've lied to me for months. You let Grace steal my memories. I will never forgive you. Any of you."

With that said, he stormed out of the library.

CHAPTER 3

Men at some time are masters of their fates; the fault, dear Brutus, is not in our stars, But in ourselves, that we are underlings. ~ Shakespeare

CHRIS awoke to a knock at his door.

He rolled to his feet and groaned. His body ached all over. His room was dark, the heavy drapes drawn against the sun.

Stepping across the clothes and clutter on his floor, he crossed the room and opened the door.

"Phoenix, what are you doing here?" he asked, rubbing the sleep from his eyes.

"It's happened," she said, her green eyes shining. "I've been elected Queen. The coronation is tonight and—what is that smell?" She pinched her nose and exaggerated a gag.

Chris shrugged. He was the smell. It had been days since he had bothered to shower.

"Anyway." A statuesque dark-haired beauty, Phoenix brushed past him, her mint green wings held high in excitement. "I know it would mean a lot to Lorna if you were there. I don't know what happened between you, but I've never seen her like this."

Chris said nothing.

Tiptoeing over a stack of dishes and empty bottles of mead cider, Phoenix pulled back one of the heavy drapes and let light filter into the room.

Chris blinked and raised his hand to shield his eyes. Was the sun always this bright?

"I'm going to contact Grace later," Phoenix added as if it were an incentive. "To see if she'll come."

"I have other plans." Chris snapped. He moved to another pile of debris beside his bed, searching for a half-full bottle he remembered dropping there.

"Really? Do they include locking yourself in your room and

wallowing in your own filth? Because that's not plans. That's an intervention waiting to happen." Phoenix picked a path back to the door. "Chris, you know you're like family to me. But Lorna *is* your family. Like it or not. Someday this is all going to blow over, and you're going to hate yourself for not going tonight. So get your stinky hide in the shower, put on some clean clothes, and come act like a big brother instead of a whiny little baby."

Phoenix grabbed the knob and slammed the door, as she exited into the hall.

* * *

PHOENIX turned just in time to walk right into the brick wall that was Lynx.

He took a step back and gave a stiff bow. "Majesty."

Phoenix could not help but think that men his size were not meant to bow. Lifting busses over their heads sure, but bowing? Not so much.

His blue-black hair had fallen into warm brown eyes. He wore his hair longer now. She fought back the urge to push the strands off his face.

"I'm not majesty yet," she said. "And to you I will always be just Phoenix."

He looked at her with those wide Unseelie eyes.

Before she could stop herself, Phoenix reached out and laid a hand on his bare shoulder. He wore only the simple tan leather pants and vest of a royal guard. The touch was familiar, but achingly formal. It was too much, or possibly too little. Either way, it hurt. So she dropped her hand back to her side.

"I wish to ask—" Lynx hesitated and cleared his throat. "That is, I request to remain as the Queen's personal guard."

Phoenix sucked in a breath. Only recently had she begun to reconnect with her old flame. Tiny embers of passion were already close to bursting into a full flame.

If he chose to remain as the Queen's guard, then the rules were clear. It was strictly forbidden for a queen to be involved with one of her guards. To say it was taboo for a Seelie Sidhe and an Unseelie Sidhe to be together was an understatement. For a queen to fraternize with lesser Fae was unthinkable.

She swallowed the melon-sized lump in her throat. She could refuse his request. That much was within her power. But doing so would infer he was not worthy. It would shame Lynx and his entire family. She wanted to slap him, to curse him for putting her in that situation. He could be with her, if only he loved her enough to set aside his stupid pride.

Phoenix stepped close to him, leaning forward so her head rested on his broad chest. It was a pain she had known before. Years ago, she begged Lynx to leave Faerie with her and help raise Pandora's daughter, Grace. He refused, choosing his duty over their love. Something inside her broke that day. She lost her faith in the idea of love and happy endings. Really, how could such a thing exist when it was denied to her?

She felt his strong arms slither around her, strong and warm. She didn't ask to be queen. It was never her desire to rule. It was Lorna who had made the nomination, much to Phoenix's surprise. And when asked to fulfill that sacred responsibility, there was only one answer.

Placing a soft kiss on the base of his neck, she pulled away and stood straight.

"Lynx," Phoenix said in her most regal voice. "You and your family have served the royal house faithfully for centuries. I would never feel safer than with you at my side."

His only reply was another formal bow.

Sweeping her long black hair over her shoulder, Phoenix turned and headed to the Fae Council chambers before Lynx saw the tears swimming in her eyes.

Philip Le Fae, Lorna and Chris' father, who had been chosen to represent the Westland and the realm of the demi-Fae, waited in the Council Chamber. Phoenix had never met the man. As the emissary to the demi-Fae, he traveled constantly. Now he stood ready to greet the new queen. He looked very little like Chris, save for the coppery brown hair. His shoulders were slender, his face more round, and his eyes more deep set.

The other advisor was Lucinda, a young and clever Fae who represented the isles and eastern borderlands. Lucinda was petite for a Fae, with wiry yellow hair and lavender and yellow striped wings. The determined set of her chin and the fact that she had an unusual gift for dispute mediation made her a good choice. Both advisors sat in deep discussion with Lorna, who was spending her last day on the throne of Faerie.

As Phoenix entered the room, the advisors bowed and took seats beside the current regent.

Queen Lorna's blue eyes were lackluster and her golden hair looked hastily coiffed. A slight droop in her golden wings just added to a general appearance of weariness.

As she took her seat opposite Queen Lorna, Phoenix could not help silently cursing Chris and his stubborn ways.

Before they could begin, there was a rap at the door.

Lynx popped his head in. "Milady, Hermes is here. He wishes to address the Queen."

Lorna motioned for him to open the door. "Show him in."

Hermes entered, for once wearing traditional Olympian robes, and offered a nod to the queen on the throne. "Lorna, I have a message from Lord Hades. He wishes you to send out the Fae known as Christopher Le Fae. I believe you know the terms of his reprieve have been violated."

"Hermes," Lorna said, getting to her feet. Her voice was thick with disdain. "Please inform Hades again that Christopher has sanctuary within the boundaries of Faerie and is not subject to the whims of an Olympian."

Hermes eyes sparkled, as he gave her a formal bow and turned to leave.

"Wait, please," Phoenix called. She moved from the table and pulled Hermes aside for a private moment. "How is Grace doing? She hasn't contacted me in months."

"Grace is…to be honest I have no idea," Hermes said quietly. "We were getting together every so often. But lately Prometheus has been keeping her from the rest of the Gods. He says she needs time to adjust, but I don't know. I have a bad feeling about the whole thing. Maybe you should speak to Prometheus directly. As the new Queen, you can demand a meeting."

"Thank you," Phoenix said. "And, Hermes, why does Hades

want Chris?"

"You'll have to ask her." Hermes motioned toward Lorna, who was being questioned in hushed tones by Philip.

Phoenix raised one eyebrow, hesitant to let the matter drop. "What aren't you telling me?"

In a flash, Hermes changed into his usual beach bum attire. He gave Phoenix an apologetic smile and then vanished.

Calmly, Phoenix turned toward the Queen. "Lorna, what's going on?"

CHAPTER 4

There are no compacts between lions and men, and
wolves and lambs have no concord. ~ Homer

AT the gates of Olympus, Prometheus waved an arm in a gesture of welcome to Phoenix, now Queen of the Fae.

Much like Faerie, Olympus existed outside the mortal realm in another dimension. After the Great War with the Titans, Zeus tried to take over the Fae lands, as well. The campaign ended in bloody stalemate. The treaty that was signed afterward still bound them today. They could not enter each other's realms without consent.

They both knew why the Fae Queen had come. Phoenix wanted to see her adopted niece and his daughter, Grace.

They faced each other with barely contained disdain. Phoenix had allowed him to enter Faerie to help Grace after the battle with Lilith last year, but his invitation had been short-lived. Since he had taken Grace to Olympus, the boundaries were now more strictly maintained.

"Phoenix," he said. "It's always a pleasure to see you."

At Prometheus side stood Apollo, who wore the same traditional Greek robe of muted gold as Prometheus.

Wearing a high-necked orange-red gown with her black hair falling over shoulders, Phoenix figured she looked like ebony on fire next to these cool golden Olympians.

Phoenix glanced behind her to where Lynx stood stoic. His face remained carefully neutral, but she could see tension in his arms. He was on edge. He didn't trust the Greeks. He made no attempt to hide that fact. Not that she could blame him.

In her opinion, the Olympians were, more often than not, untrustworthy and deceptive. And now they had Grace. With her powers growing so rapidly, there was the potential of Grace becoming very dangerous weapon in the enemy's hands.

Lynx must have been thinking the same thing. As their eyes connected, his mouth tensed, as if he held back words best left unsaid. With the barest tilt of her head, Phoenix tried to express her trust in Grace.

Phoenix turned back to face Prometheus. "I've come to see Grace."

"Ah, right to the point, as always," he said with a dry laugh. "Monarchy has yet to temper your warrior's tongue, I see."

"And I see you being kicked to the bottom of the Olympian food chain hasn't improved your manners," Phoenix countered, instantly regretting having let him get her so riled.

Prometheus' eyes flashed red for an instant and then faded back to green. He expelled a tight breath. Turning to Apollo, he waved his hand.

"Will you please go see if Grace has a moment?" he asked the sun god.

With a flick of his shoulder-length yellow curls, Apollo stepped inside the archway that was the entrance to Olympus and vanished.

"Not going to invite me in?" Phoenix asked.

"Ah, I don't think that would be prudent," Prometheus replied. "We've had our differences in the past. Though we've come to an agreement, albeit an uneasy one for the sake of my daughter, I doubt some of the other Gods will be so forgiving."

"I stand by the decisions that were made," Phoenix added. "The Olympians had been abusing their powers for far too long."

"So the Fae went running to the Mother to tattle on us. Yes, some of our family did grow corrupt." His eyes flashed red again. "But it was our place to deal with them, not yours."

Lynx took a step forward from Phoenix's side, his hand on his halberd.

As if on cue, Apollo reappeared between Prometheus and Lynx, glowing balls of energy ready in each hand.

"I'd like to see you try, Sidhe," Apollo challenged with a growl.

"Enough," Prometheus commanded with a hand on Apollo's

sun-kissed shoulder.

"Grace is resting," Apollo said, after allowing his energy weapons to reabsorb into his palms.

Prometheus nodded, his gaze never moving from the Fae Queen. "I'm sorry, Phoenix. Grace has been training hard and her body is still adjusting to the magic of Olympus. She must be allowed to rest. I will tell her you came by."

"Not good enough. I want to see her now, for myself." Phoenix paused. "I need to see that she's safe."

"And you suppose what?" Prometheus asked. "That I am holding her captive here? As if I could. Grace left Faerie of her own accord and came home to be near her family. I will tell her that you would like to see her. But whether she chooses to see you or not will be her decision."

Phoenix's hands balled into fists at her sides, as she fought to control her violent urges. "Fine," she said through gritted teeth. "Tell her I came. And ask her to come see me, please."

Phoenix motioned for Lynx. As they turned to leave, she paused to say one more thing. "Prometheus, do the Olympians truly blame us for what the Great Mother decided?"

Prometheus hesitated. "To a degree, yes. Wouldn't you, if the roles were reversed? But it is of no matter now. The situation is being rectified."

"What do you mean, rectified?"

Prometheus gave a sly smile and shrugged. "Only that we are rediscovering our true purpose."

"Which is?" Phoenix asked.

Ignoring the question, Prometheus gave a half-bow and vanished.

* * *

PROMETHEUS and Apollo walked together down the main path toward Apollo's temple. Not having a temple of his own, Prometheus had taken up residence in the old temple of Ares which was just next door.

"Do you think the Fae will try to interfere?" Apollo asked.

Prometheus laughed and clapped his fellow Olympian on the

back. "I'm counting on it, old friend."

Apollo waved and headed toward his own temple.

Prometheus continued on past the temple of Ares and made his way to where his daughter lay sleeping.

Creeping into her room, he watched sleep soundly with her red hair flared around her like a fiery halo. She had made very few changes to the temple he prepared for her. The most noticeable was the addition of a luxurious bathroom. Immortals didn't need such things, but she assured him it was necessary for her relaxation.

He frowned, moving an errant strand of hair from her face. She was lovely, much like her mother had been. For a moment, his heart was heavy, a lead balloon inside his chest. He looked at her side table covered with pictures held in shining silver frames. One was Phoenix and Grace playing at the beach. The other was Pandora and a human man holding Grace as an infant. How he wished he could have known Grace as a child. Was she always so headstrong? Or had she adopted that defiance from her *Aunt* Phoenix? Grace had been a beautiful infant. That much he knew from the photographs. He tried to remember that she was here now, but it did little to soothe him. He longed for a child of his own. To love and teach and raise. Someone who would be totally devoted to him, the way Pandora was at one time. Alas, Pandora had grown to hate him and Phoenix had helped hide his daughter from him.

Reaching down, Prometheus slid a small sapphire necklace from around Grace's neck and held it in his hands. He had created the stone from one of her own tears and given it to her as a gift. It was fashioned in the first moment she accepted him as her father and held remnants of those emotions. Closing his fingers tightly around the stone, he closed his eyes and focused all his power into the amulet, pushing energy into the necklace and through the necklace into her. With his other hand, he withdrew the Eye of Hera from his toga. Laying it gently on her forehead, he drew her powers out of her body.

He pulled her powers into the orb and then replaced them with his diminished ones. Using the necklace, they were joined in a circle of power. Both of them glowing like stars in the night, sparks of energy crackling in the air around them. Only the small blue stone of the amulet kept her from waking, from feeling the stinging pain of the process.

As he cycled power between them, Prometheus whispered.

And Grace dreamed.

CHAPTER 5

She nourishes the poison in her veins and
is consumed by a secret fire. ~ Virgil

GRACE groaned and rolled onto her back.

Pungent sulfur permeated the air as she dragged in each aching breath. With great effort, she opened her eyes but saw only rolling shades of gray. Somewhere in a distant part of her mind, she realized this was not just another bad dream. Static played in the background of her ears, just behind the dull ringing.

She stood, coughing against the smoke being drawn into her lungs.

Sounds of combat came from every direction, but she could not see past her own outstretched hand. Lights flashed around her, illuminating the area enough for Grace to make out the vague outlines of people fighting, some with halberds and other with energy blasts. It was like watching shadow puppets on a white sheet as she tried to focus on the sounds, tried to make sense of the strange vision.

A familiar voice got her attention.

"No!" Prometheus cried out from somewhere to her left. The single word was followed by a blood-curdling scream.

Grace ran to the sound, breaking through dense fog and stepping into the partial light.

There she saw Phoenix garbed neck-to-toe in thick green leather. Her hair was pulled back in a tight black braid and her face smeared with blood. She stood over Prometheus, swinging a halberd in each hand.

"Give me the Eye of Hera!" Phoenix demanded.

"I cannot!" Prometheus yelled hoarsely, holding up a hand to shield himself. "The Fae will never rule over the Gods!"

Phoenix laughed. It was a bitter sound. Something Grace had

never heard from her aunt. With a swing of her axe, Phoenix cut a deep gash across Prometheus' midsection. The smell of it hit Grace like a truck, riding over even the strong smell of sulfur. The gag reflex in the back of Grace's throat hitched and she fought to swallow back the sick bile rising into her mouth.

"We will not allow you to be as you once were," Phoenix said. "And you don't have Grace here to protect you this time!"

"What have you done with my daughter?" Prometheus cried.

Behind him, Chris stepped out of the shadows with a fierce grin on his face and Grace's sapphire necklace dangling from his blood soaked hand.

Grace lunged forward, but found the thin white sheet from her bed inside her Olympian temple was tangled around her legs. She fell onto the hard floor of her room. Heart pounding, she lay there for a several minutes, catching her breath.

"Grace?" Prometheus called from the entryway. "Are you all right?"

She stood, extricating herself from the sheet and smoothing her hair as best she could with her fingers. "I'm fine. Just a minute."

She changed into a clean set of loose crimson pants and a white tank top. Grabbing her brush, she quickly set her red hair into a tight ponytail. Stepping into her newly added bathroom, she brushed her teeth and washed her face. She didn't technically need to do these things, one small perk of immortality, but the routine was comfortable and felt good.

"Okay, I'm decent," she called. "You can come in."

Usually, the Gods just walked in on each other. She had convinced Prometheus to announce himself before entering her bedroom.

He strode in confidently, clad only in white cotton slacks, his white wings brushing the floor.

Grace was still adjusting to the fact that most of the time the Olympians liked to run around almost naked. On Eros, it was just yummy eye candy. On her father, it made her cringe.

"Are you well?" he asked, manifesting a tray of fruit on her bed. "I heard you cry out."

Had she screamed? She could not remember.

"It was just a vision," she said with a sigh.

"Are you certain it wasn't a dream?" He sat in the lounge and helped himself to some berries.

"I don't think so. When I have visions, there is this sort of static. I don't get that when I'm just dreaming."

"I see. And what was this vision?"

Grace picked up an apple and took a bite, swallowing slowly. She didn't want to share what she had seen. Not with him.

"Oh, nothing important," she replied with a nonchalant shrug.

"Well, what would you like to do today?" he asked casually.

Phoenix would have picked up on Grace's lie immediately, because they were so close. She could not decide if it was just that Prometheus didn't know her well enough to see through the lie, or if he was just content not to push her for the truth.

"Actually, I've been thinking of going to see Phoenix."

Prometheus stiffened.

"What?" she demanded.

"Grace, some things have changed since you left Faerie."

Grace's first thought was of Chris. "What?" she asked, leaning forward.

"The Fae have elected a new queen. Phoenix."

Grace sat back, puzzled. "What happened to Lorna? Is she okay?"

"Lorna is fine, I assure you. It was simply the end of her term. The Fae voted and Phoenix was elected to take her place."

Grace held her breath, trying to calculate dates in her brain and coming up with nothing. "How long have I been here? In real time."

He smiled. "I do enjoy how you still refer to the human world as the 'real' place. As if everything else is but a dream. To answer your question, it is February in the human world. What has been only weeks here, has been months there."

Grace just nodded. Months. Months had passed for Phoenix. She needed to see her aunt and soon.

"I do think, however, that you might want to postpone your

visit a bit longer," Prometheus said cryptically.

"Why?"

"I didn't want to have to tell you this." He sighed. "Phoenix came to see me yesterday."

"What? She was here? Didn't she want to see me?"

He shifted uncomfortably. "She was here on official business, you must understand. News reached her that we were considering reunifying the Council of the Gods. She came to deliver a warning."

"What kind of warning?"

"Grace, you must understand that there has been mistrust and prejudice between the Fae and the Olympians since the fall of the Titans," he explained. "Our truce has always been an uncomfortable one. When our powers were reduced and our numbers dwindled, we were, for the first time, on an even playing field, so to speak. They are reluctant to allow us to do anything that might upset that balance. They feel, threatened by us."

"Well, that's stupid." Grace fumed, folding her arms across her chest. "It's not like we're plotting to take over or anything. We just want to be united, so we can take care of each other and humanity. What's so wrong with that?"

Prometheus patted her knee. "Nothing is wrong with that. And they will eventually see that they can trust us. It just may take some time."

Grace shook her head. "I think I should go. Explain things to Phoenix. She'll listen to me."

"Perhaps you're right." Prometheus' voice had a bitter edge to it. "Being raised outside both realms, you might be the best emissary. Before you leave, I suggest we call together the remaining Gods and work out the fine points of reunification."

"Why the tone?"

"I still haven't forgiven Phoenix for keeping you from me all those years. I had a right to know about my own child."

They never talked about this. It was the past. They had moved on, or so she thought.

"She was only doing what mom wanted her to do," Grace said, defending Phoenix.

Prometheus huffed. "So she says. It just doesn't make sense to me. What would you have missed out on, what would you have been denied by being raised here? Nothing I can fathom."

Grace opened her mouth, but then closed it. As always, thoughts of Chris were on the tip of her tongue. She once believed it was their destiny to be together. Being wrong was still more painful than she was ready to admit.

"I'm sure she had her reasons," Grace said.

"Her reasons are not my own, nor do they impress me," Prometheus said, showing real anger toward Pandora and Phoenix. With a resigned breath, he stood and held out his hand to Grace. "Come, daughter. Let us put a call to our brethren. The council meets again."

CHAPTER 6

There is nothing like dream to create the future. Utopia
today, flesh and blood tomorrow. ~ Victor Hugo

THERE were more Gods in attendance than Grace expected. She insisted they invite all demi-gods and half-gods, except the few in the human world with no abilities or connections to their godly parents. Only one set of twins in their fifties fit that category. Their father was Apollo, and they had no idea that Greek Gods even existed, much less that their biological father was one. So Grace agreed to leave the twins to their mortal lives.

All in all, there were fifteen Olympians in attendance, including Grace. Even Pan was there. He had shed his normal goat form for a human one, though his scruffy goatee and white-gray hair still made him look more animal than human.

Hades also answered the call, though he didn't look happy about it. He and Persephone, wife of Hades, talked in hushed tones with Eris, the Goddess of Discord.

There were only two new faces, Calliope and Chance.

Calliope was a Muse, but welcome nonetheless. Today she appeared in her normal form, tall and thin with short ginger red hair and dark blue eyes. But she could change appearance at will and even become invisible when it suited her.

Chance was a half-god, but no one seemed to know who his parents were or how old he really was. He stood stiffly in a simple pair of jeans and a navy blue T-shirt. Hermes had found him working as a blackjack dealer in Las Vegas.

"If you would, take your positions along the outer ring," Prometheus asked over the murmuring. He motioned to the floor and the thin gold line that circled the room.

They complied, looking very formal.

Prometheus motioned to Grace.

She drew in a deep breath and closed her eyes. She reached down inside herself, into the abyss that held her powers. She tapped into it, letting it flow up into her, filling her with crackling energy. The ground shook as she focused. Slowly, the ground behind each god cracked and a new throne spit up from the earth. Each throne was plain granite.

As the Gods took their seats, the chairs began to change.

Hades sat and his chair turned black, flowing with spirals of blood-red emeralds that curled up from the base. Tall, dark and dangerous-looking in an expensive business suit, he matched his new throne.

It was the same with each god, their new thrones absorbing and taking on characteristics from those that sat in them. All except for Prometheus' throne, that remained gray-white.

Grace opened her eyes and swept a glance around the room before taking her own seat. As soon as she touched it, she felt it come alive. The granite morphed into golden sandstone that shimmered in the torchlight.

"Why have we been gathered?" Hades demanded.

"We've been separate too long, my brothers and sisters," Prometheus said with an air of authority. "The time has come to reclaim our destiny. United as one, we can use our combined powers to once more find purpose in our existence."

A murmur went out among the crowd.

"We've been reprimanded," Hermes interjected in an even tone. "Many of us have little power left. I, for one, would not seek to incur the Mother's wrath again."

"It is true," Hephaestus whispered, managing to make himself heard from within the gray hood hiding a face disfigured on just one side. The hunchbacked God of the Forge shifted on his throne. "But perhaps there is something to be said for having a purpose again. What good is a hammer, if not to be used to forge a sword?"

"We were punished, because we had grown selfish and lax in our mandate," Prometheus said. "We were created to be leaders, protectors to mankind. We failed in that mission."

"The humans turned from us long ago," Eros snapped,

folding his arms across his bare ebony chest. Raven wings lay against his back, as he sat on his throne of red marble. His bald head shone in the flickering torchlight. "They no longer praise us for our aid, choosing instead to glorify themselves. Is it any wonder so many of us stopped answering their calls?"

"Glory?" Grace asked, jumping into the conversation. Her voice was tight with frustration. "Is that all you cared about? Getting the credit?"

"Little cousin, you must understand." Apollo's voice was gentle, but there was an edge to his words. "For centuries we were worshiped. They sang stories about us around fires. Left offerings at our temples. Then they abandoned us, turning their eyes elsewhere. We were left to watch, as they defiled our temples and tried to remove our very existence from history. Even today we are thought of as nothing but archaic myths. We were betrayed by the ones we loved most."

Hades grip tightened on the arms of his throne. "I don't know what any of this has to do with me. My purpose is always the same. Death is the only constant in the universe. You bicker about things that do not pertain to me and my kingdom."

Grace swallowed a lump in her throat. Hades scared the living crap out of her and deep down she hated him. No, that was not entirely true. She hated death itself, not the person before her. But for the sake of her people, she must bury the hatchet with Hades, even if she secretly wished it was in his back.

"Hades, you're right," Grace said as humbly as she could manage. "You're one of the oldest and wisest Gods. We asked you here for the benefit of your knowledge. If we are to be united in a single, noble purpose, we need you with us,"

Hades looked content. "Of course. What 'noble purpose' did you imagine?"

Grace looked to her father, who motioned for her to proceed. "Your original purpose was to guide, teach, and protect humanity," she said. "I suggest we begin that again. This time without making ourselves known. The reward isn't in receiving glory, but in serving others. When you give without thought of getting something in return, it is an act of pure love. I believe you loved the mortals once. I think we should build that again. With this, the new Council of Olympus, we can finally do what we were created to do. Together."

"It is a noble purpose, indeed, that you dream of, Grace," Hephaestus said in a kind voice.

Hermes shook his head. "We've been forbidden to interfere with the lives of mortals. We had our opportunity to do good. We failed."

"The world no longer needs us," Eros said.

"Speak for yourself," Hades growled.

Pan stood and cast a wary glance at Hermes. "I agree with my father."

Eris flipped her long dark hair over her shoulder. "I, for one, have no desire to serve mortals. What are they to me?"

"Caution, sister," Apollo said with a frown. "It is that attitude that earned our castigation."

Grace scanned their faces and found one that looked more reflective. "Chance, what do you think?"

Chance sat forward in his throne, which had taken on the appearance of a high-backed barstool. "I'm not sure what to say. I'm not even sure why I'm here. I have no place in this council, no parents who claim me. I've been scraping out an existence with the mortals for longer than I care to remember. My loyalties are to them, not this council."

"Do you think humanity could benefit from our help?" Grace asked, intrigued.

He thought about it for a minute, folding his fingers under his chin and resting his elbows on his legs. "Perhaps. Humanity is flawed and fragile. On one hand, they are capable of such beauty. On the other, they seem to crave violence. They will not be ruled by Gods or men. But if, as Grace suggested, you remain in the shadows, then yes. Help, guidance, protection. Humans need these things."

"And who among us shall rule this council?" Eris asked, glaring at Grace.

"Grace is the most powerful among us," Prometheus said.

"But too young and undisciplined to lead," Hades added.

Pan nodded in agreement. "Grace has marvelous potential, but it is yet to be seen if she can truly be trusted." He paused, stroking his gray goatee. "She was raised by the Fae."

"What's that supposed to mean?" Grace leaned forward on her throne. She had done everything for them, left everyone she cared about and was bending over backwards to help them get their act together. Did they still not trust her?

Prometheus gestured with his hand for her to calm down. "It is not an insult to you, daughter. It was merely a stated fact. The Fae have long been at odds with the Olympians. Had you been raised here by your true family, you would understand and know us better."

Grace sat still, fuming.

"Yes, it is a reasonable fear to believe your loyalties might be divided," Eris practically hissed.

Grace wanted to slap Eris. And to think, it was not long ago she had saved Eris' life, nearly dying in the process.

"It is true that Grace is powerful," Hermes added. "But it is also true she lacks control of her powers. Her loyalties, however, I do not doubt."

Grace gave Hermes a thankful nod. "I understand your concerns. And to be frank, I don't want to rule anyone. I don't know most of you, and you don't know me. I suggest something different. A democracy."

Hades laughed. "Yes, that worked out so well for the Romans."

A few Gods nodded. Some just smirked.

"I like the idea of everyone getting a vote," Hephaestus added in his quiet voice.

"For a democracy to work there must still be one with the power to end disputes," Apollo chimed in. "In case you haven't noticed, our numbers are even. Fourteen. We need one who can be a tie-breaker, if the need arises."

"Prometheus is the logical choice," Hephaestus said. "He is the God of Foresight. His abilities are uniquely suited to foresee any problems that may arise from any decision."

Grace shifted, looking at her father. Never once had he

mentioned having visions, as she did. She had been under the impression her visions were inherited from her mother, who had been infected by a bite from the demon of Foresight when she opened the forbidden urn. Was it possible she received her ability from both sides?

"I agree," Apollo said in a firm voice. "Prometheus would be a good choice."

"I, for one, think it should be me," Hades argued, sitting straight. "I am very skilled at passing judgment."

A murmur of voices roiled through the room.

Prometheus stood, holding up his hands for silence. "Brothers and sisters, there is only one fair way to decide. We'll meet back here in one week's time and put the matter to a vote. Majority carries. In the event of a tie, we'll find another way to choose. A lottery, perhaps. Thank you all for coming!"

With a series of flashes they disappeared, leaving only Prometheus, Grace, and Hermes. Hermes approached Grace where she sat beside her father, waiting until everyone was gone so she could question him about his powers.

"Grace, your aunt has asked me to relay a message. She would like you to come for a visit. She needs to speak with you." Hermes tipped his head. "As does Lorna."

Why would Lorna need to see her? Her stomach flipped. Hermes eyes flashed gold as Grace opened her mouth. She paused. Desperately wanting to know if Chris was all right, she swallowed the question. The look Hermes was giving her was a warning. It said clearly not to ask any questions right now.

"I'll leave soon. I just need to talk to my father for a moment," Grace answered, trying to keep her voice from betraying her concern.

Hermes bowed his head and vanished.

"Grace? Is there something wrong?" Prometheus asked.

"I'm sure it's nothing. I needed to go see Phoenix anyway. I didn't realize your powers were anything like mine."

"In my prime, I was able to see possible futures," informed Prometheus. "Nothing like the visions you and your mother have. It was almost an overly sharp sense of direction. I could tell where a decision or choice would lead."

"Do you still have that ability?" Grace asked.

"To some degree, but lesser than before."

She laughed. "So how do you see all this turning out?"

He tilted his head, as if trying to see a great distance. "I never underestimate our ability to put our own pettiness above doing the right thing. We are selfish creatures. Zeus used threats to keep the Gods loyal. It's why the Eye of Hera was created. So he could maintain control."

"Forcing them to do the right thing is just as bad as forcing them to do the wrong thing," Grace added. "I want them to join us because they want to, because they believe in the mission. Not because they are afraid of us."

Prometheus covered her hand with his. "Sometimes, I see so much of your mother in you."

"Do you think she'd be proud? Do you think I'm doing the right thing?"

He stood and kissed Grace on the forehead. "I don't know what your mother would say, if she were here. But I know that I am very proud to be your father."

Then he vanished,

Grace sat alone in a chamber of empty thrones. Could she really convince them to unite?

After a few minutes of reflection, Grace flashed back to her room. She changed into her burgundy corset and full skirt that was her typical attire in Faerie. With one last look around, she imagined standing outside the entrance to Faerie that lay on Goat Island in Washington.

In a blink, she faced the deep green water that filled the old cistern. She took a moment to breathe in the heavy, salty air of the Puget Sound. Above her, a Bald Eagle cried out in warning as it dove into the trees. The sound sent a shiver up her spine.

She stood on the edge of the murky pool. Feeling quite silly for being spooked by a bird, she leapt into the portal that would take her back to Aletheia.

CHAPTER 7

*Years of love have been forgot, in the hatred
of a minute.*~ Edgar Allan Poe

ALETHEIA was beautiful, as always.

Grace wandered down winding cobblestone paths. She could have just blinked herself into the Fae palace, but she had missed this place and wanted to take her time. The small market was busy as people brought their wares to trade.

Olympus was beautiful in its own way, but also cold and empty. It had no adorable children whose playful laughter danced on the wind, and no chatting ladies who wove tapestries in the main square. On Olympus everyone kept to themselves and, other than the musical fountains, it was always quiet. No birds sang. No wind blew in the trees. On Olympus there was never darkness, just constant bland daylight and stillness. By contrast, Aletheia was full of life. Just walking through it brought a smile to her face. Like a battery that had been drained, she let it settle inside, warming her.

A familiar voice startled her from a pleasant stupor.

"Grace, is that you?"

It was Luna, the second half of Chris' twin sisters. She carried a basket of fruits in one hand and balanced a bundle of cloth in the other. Golden hair flew in her blue eyes, and her pale gold wings fluttered as she struggled.

"Luna! How are you?" Grace realized it was not a bundle of cloth Luna carried, but a tiny baby. The baby cooed, clutching its mother's loose hair with an impossibly tiny fist.

"Oh!" Grace gasped. "You had the baby!"

Of course. I've been away for months. Grace shook her head, feeling stupid for the second time that day.

"Yes, this is little Liam," Luna said with a smile. "Would you like to hold him?"

Grace might have said no, only because she never held such a small person and was half-terrified she might drop him, but she noticed Luna struggling with the fruit basket and relented.

"Of course," she said cautiously.

Sure, Grace knew the mechanics of holding a baby, but after a failed school project that involved a raw egg and her first and last failing grade, she was a little spooked. Still, she held out her arms and took the squirming bundle.

The moment she wrapped her arms around him, she froze. "Uh, Luna, wings?"

Luna chuckled. "No. No wings yet. They come in at three years old."

Relieved, Grace clutched the child to her chest and slid her finger down his cheek. "He's so cute," she said softly as his small hand wrapped around her finger and tried to pull it to his mouth.

When he opened his little eyes and looked up at her, Grace's mouth fell open. His eyes were big and round, deep blue with flakes of gold in them. Just like his uncle's. Just like Chris. It made Grace's chest constrict.

"How are things going?" Grace asked, not pulling her eyes from the tiny baby.

"Well, things are good," Luna said with noticeable hesitance.

This made Grace look up.

"Chris hasn't been feeling well," Luna added. "He's been depressed. Angry. I don't know what happened."

But Grace knew. The last time she seen him, he said he loved her and she ran away. She had left without bothering to say goodbye. He had every right to be angry.

Trying to plaster on a fake smile, Grace handed Liam back to his mother. "Maybe I'll go see him while I'm here," she offered.

Luna nodded. "That would be great. I'm sure he would love to see you."

Doubt it, Grace thought.

"Take care, Luna," Grace murmured softly.

"You too, Grace."

Grace turned away. Enough procrastinating.

With a blink, she stood inside the palace just beyond the tall doors that lead into the Queen's chambers. She knocked twice.

Lynx popped his head out the door. Looking surprised, he allowed Grace to enter.

"Is Phoenix here?" she asked.

"This way." Lynx smiled and motioned for her to follow him.

He led her to a chamber, where Phoenix sat at a small round table going over papers with two other Fae that Grace didn't know.

Phoenix's head popped up. "Grace!" Smiling, she got to her feet and then turned to her advisers. "Thank you. We'll go over the rest of these later."

After the advisors had left the chamber, Phoenix walked over and pulled Grace into a tight hug.

"How are you?" Grace asked, hugging her back. "I've missed you so much!"

"I'm fine. Oh, Grace, so much has happened. I tried to come see you."

"I heard you came by," Grace said. "Sorry I missed you. But I'm here now. What's all this I hear about you being queen? How did that happen?"

Phoenix sighed. Taking Grace by the arm, she led her into a room filled with large chairs and couches. She sat, motioning for Grace to join her.

"It was unexpected," Phoenix explained. "Lorna nominated me when her term was over. Truth be told, I didn't even vote for myself. Ruling the Fae was a responsibility I never wanted. But when your people ask you to serve, you don't say no."

Grace watched Phoenix's nose wrinkle as she spoke, a gesture her aunt always made when faced with unpleasant tasks, like taking out the trash or scrubbing the toilet.

"They couldn't have chosen a better leader," Grace said in her most reassuring voice.

Phoenix leaned forward, speaking around Grace to Lynx who stood stiffly at the door. "Lynx, please go find Lorna and bring her here. We need to speak with her."

Lynx bowed and stalked out of the chamber.

When they were alone, Phoenix squeezed one of Grace's hands. "I need to know what's going on in Olympus."

"Why?" Grace asked, raising an eyebrow.

"We have word that they are reforming the Council of the Gods."

"That's true," Grace admitted. "We are."

Phoenix stood, her long golden gown swishing as she moved. "Grace, you can't let them do that."

"Why not?"

"Because the Great Goddess has forbidden it," Phoenix replied. "She destroyed it for a reason, Grace."

"I know they were punished for being corrupt and selfish. But we're trying to fix that." Grace didn't understand. Why was Phoenix being unreasonable? "All we want to do is help people."

"It's not your place, Grace. That's the Guardians' job," Phoenix said with a dismissive wave of her hand.

"Why? Don't you think this would be better? Right now the Gods just wander around doing nothing. For eternity. Isn't it better for them to use what little power they still have to do some good in the world?"

"It might start out that way, Grace, but how long until they are back to their old ways?" Phoenix's tone was soothing, almost patronizing. "They are too selfish to care about anything but themselves, don't you see that?"

"Don't talk down to me like I'm some kind of child." Grace got to her feet. "They are my family."

"No, I'm your family," Phoenix corrected her. "You seem to have forgotten that when you took off without bothering to say goodbye."

"Please! You were so busy playing Romeo and Juliet with Lynx. You didn't have time for me anymore. If not for Prometheus, I would not know of your coronation." Grace's argument was a weak one, and she knew it. When Grace struck her bargain with Hades, it made it hard to talk to her aunt. Overnight, the one person she would normally lean on became someone she could not afford to see. Phoenix would have seen right through her, so Grace did the only thing she could. She avoided her.

"Hey, you shut me out a long time before you left," Phoenix said. "What was up with that?"

Phoenix was not as oblivious as Grace had hoped.

Grace clenched her jaw and decided to proceed with as much as honesty as she was allowed by Hades bargain, which was not much. "I didn't want to. I was going through stuff. Stuff I couldn't talk to you about."

"That's a load of crap, Grace. You've always been able to talk to me about anything."

Grace shook her head. *Not this.*

"And even now you aren't going to tell me the truth, are you?" Phoenix spat.

"I can't. I'm keeping a promise." Grace sank back into the soft chair, hoping it would swallow her whole.

"Whatever," Phoenix said, turning away.

"Don't you *whatever* me! You did the same thing remember? All those years you lied to me and kept me away from my father."

"I didn't know who he was." Phoenix turned back to defend herself, her hand going to her chest.

"So you say. But I'm starting to think you'd do just about anything to keep me away from Prometheus."

"It was your mother's decision. I just respected her wishes. I kept you safe." Although Phoenix's tone was calmer, it held a hint of bitterness.

"You kept me hidden away like a dirty secret. You lied to me my whole life about who I was, what I was." Grace's blood began to boil. The rage inside her tried to claw its way out. She snapped her mouth shut to keep from saying something she could not take back.

As Grace struggled with herself, the door swung open and Lorna strode into the chamber. Grace almost didn't recognize the former queen, clad now in a simple white dress with her yellow-gold hair pulled back in delicate braids.

"Grace, I'm so glad you've come," Lorna said. "Something terrible has happened."

"What? Is Chris all right?" Grace leapt to her feet, all her rage slipping away in a breath.

"Physically, yes," Lorna replied. "For now anyway. Grace, he knows."

"Knows what exactly?" Grace asked, her heart pounding.

"Everything."

Stunned, Grace fell back into her seat. How could this have happened? She had been so careful. The only reason she left Faerie was to keep Chris safe, to keep him from finding out the truth. Had all of that pain and anguish been for nothing?

Grace tried to process the news. "What do you mean by everything? How is that possible?" Her gaze narrowed on Lorna. "Did you tell him?"

"No, of course not," Lorna swore, falling into the nearest chair. "Apparently, he followed you into the Hall of Memory the last time you were here. Then he went back later on his own. He confronted me, demanding the truth."

Grace's mind reeled. When was the last time she was at The Hall of Memory? It was before they captured Samael, before she left for Olympus. Oh Gods, what did she do?

"Grace, you need to tell me what happened," Phoenix said, resting a hand on Grace's shoulder.

Grace let the truth stumble out of her mouth without a thought. What was the point of keeping the lie now? It rolled off her tongue in a flood.

"Chris died," Grace explained, her voice cracking. "I made a deal with Hades to bring him back. But there was a price. Hades took away Chris' memory of me. I know you don't remember, but we loved each other, so much."

"But you didn't even meet him until after you destroyed Lilith," Phoenix said, confused.

"No, that's the memory they changed. Chris saved me at graduation. You and he brought me here." Grace struggled to breathe, to speak. "I was forbidden to tell anyone. If Chris ever found out or if I broke my word, Hades would take him back to the Underworld. That was the deal. I wanted to tell you so badly, but I couldn't." She doubled over, clutching her waist.

"But later, here, you and Chris were getting so close,"

Phoenix said.

"It was my fault. I couldn't stay away from him. I know I should have—" Grace broke off. What could she say? She was selfish. Weak. Broken.

Phoenix thought for a minute. "And you couldn't tell me this, but you could tell Lorna?"

Grace shook her head where it rested on her knees. "Lorna was there. She and James helped me get to Hades. Look, it's a long story. I'm so sorry. I couldn't tell you. Or anyone. And the more time I spent with Chris, the harder it was to keep lying to him. I came so close to blowing everything. So I left."

Grace got up and sat beside Lorna, wrapping an arm around her shoulders.

"I thought you left because of something I did," Phoenix whispered.

"Of course not. But I couldn't be with him, and I couldn't talk to you. I just felt so alone."

"That's why Hades wants Chris," Phoenix said, connecting the dots.

Lorna looked up and nodded.

"What?" Grace asked. "Hades doesn't have Chris yet?"

Lorna shook her head no. "He sent Hermes to tell us to send Chris out of Faerie."

"Of course," Grace said, relieved. "Hades magic doesn't work here. Chris is safe as long as he doesn't leave."

If he remembers then maybe we could be together, she thought as the wheels in her brain finally clicked into place. Even if they could never leave Faerie, they could at least be together.

"I have to see him," Grace said.

"Maybe you shouldn't," Lorna warned. "Grace, he's taking it very hard that he can't leave Faerie. He was so upset that we had to lie to him."

"That's why I need to talk to him. I can explain. Make things right." Grace bounded off the chair. "I'll be back soon."

In a blink, she was on her way to find Chris.

CHAPTER 8

*Know that when I hate you it is because I love you to a point
of passion that unhinges my soul.* ~ Julie de Lespinasse

CHRIS was not in his room or at the waterfall.

Grace had almost given up looking for him. Then she
thought of one last place he might be.

When she got to the Hall of Memory, the doors were open
but the room was dark, darker than usual. If it was not for the
subtle sound of someone breathing, she would have left,
assuming it to be empty.

"Hello?" she asked into the darkness. "Is anyone in here?"

Instantly, the wall torches sprang to life, illuminating the
temple. Chris sat cross-legged on the floor in the center of the
room. He was gaunt and pale, as if he hadn't slept in weeks. His
dark blue eyes were bloodshot, and his coppery brown hair hung
in tangles. His blue and gold wings drooped on the dusty floor.

Cautiously, she moved to his side and sat beside him.

He watched her with wary eyes.

"Chris, are you okay?" she asked.

He continued to stare at her.

Grace didn't know what to say or how to begin. She wanted
nothing more than to fall into his arms and let the truth gush
from her like a geyser. But seeing him like this pulled her up
short. Then she remembered what Luna told her. Chris was
angry. She could feel it coming off him in ripples.

A few silent seconds passed.

"Luna and Lorna are worried about you," Grace said. "I'm
worried about you."

She wanted to reach out to him, but didn't dare. His face held
a hard and cold expression. It was a look she hoped never to see
upon his face again. He reminded her of a wild animal caught in a

trap and waiting for someone to spring the net.

With a loud exhale, he looked away from her. "What do you care?"

His words were like a dagger in her heart. The pain was sharp and immediate.

"I love you," Grace whispered, hoping he would look at her. Hoping he would feel the truth of her words.

Instead, he snorted. "You left."

"I had to," she said, swallowing a lump in her throat.

"No," he ground out. "I saw what you saw, in here. I know the truth. But I don't feel it. I don't remember it. What I remember is the lie."

"How did you find out?"

"Before you left, I snuck in here with you," Chris admitted. "I wanted to convince you to stay with me. But something made me hide, made me watch. Maybe it was instinct. Or maybe I was just trying to figure out why you kept pushing me away with one hand while pulling me along with the other."

She flinched at his words, feeling guilt like ice in the marrow of her bones.

"That day I came to your room," he continued, "I wanted to confront you about what I saw. I wanted to be angry, but you looked so lost, so alone. I should have told you, but I lost my nerve. I wasn't sure if what I saw in here was real or some trick. And then you left. And I went looking for answers. Lorna and Hermes finally told me the truth."

"I understand if you hate me," Grace said, looking away. "I hate myself sometimes. Most of the time actually. But I just couldn't leave you there. I wanted you to have a chance at life, even if it meant I couldn't be a part of it."

"You lied to me," he said in a strangled voice. "Every day you lied to me. You let me believe you lost someone you loved."

"I did lose someone I loved. I lost you." Grace's vision blurred. Just when she thought she had reached a place where there were no more tears, they came back in full force. There were always more tears, she realized.

"Did you?" Anger had slipped into Chris' voice. "Love me,

that is. You bargained away my memories easily enough."

"I never stopped loving you," she vowed.

He brushed a strand of hair off her face. He was looking at her now, his eyes shiny with unshed tears of his own.

"I loved you," Chris said in a strained voice. "I don't remember loving you before. But when I met you that day at the waterfall, I fell in love with you. We could have been happy together. Why did you fight me? Why did you leave?"

The guilt was crushing her. Stifling her. Grace thought telling him the truth would lift a weight from her shoulders, but it didn't. The sad reality was sometimes the lie hurt less than the truth.

She cupped his hand with her own and turned her face to place a kiss in his palm. "I hated lying to you. It killed me inside. But I couldn't stay away from you. I came so close to telling you the truth. I slipped up so many times. I knew if I stayed, it was just a matter of time until I wouldn't be able to lie anymore, or before I screwed everything up again. I didn't want to lose you. Not again." A tear slid down her cheek into his hand.

A few more minutes passed in silence, though it felt like an eternity to Grace.

"And James?" Chris asked.

Grace released his hand. "Please. There's never been anyone for me but you. There never will be. You have to understand, I only went to Olympus to keep you safe. Safe from me. I'm just not good for you. I keep getting you killed."

"You went to Hades to get me back," he said with a half-formed smile. "That was dangerous."

"You have no idea," Grace said remembering just how close she came not to making it out at all. "But the deal with Hades, it wasn't even about you. Not really. He wanted to punish me by taking away the thing I loved most. So he took you. James made me realize that it was better for both of us if I stayed away from you. It was selfish of me to spend all that time with you, to lie to you all those months. But I need it. I needed you. But it was bad for you. Dangerous. I kept slipping up, saying too much and having to lie to cover it up. So I left, to keep you safe."

Chris laid his hand over Grace's where it rested on her knee.

A dozen emotions danced on his face as Grace watched. His brow furrowed and his jaw relaxed into a sad frown.

"I understand, Grace. It still hurts, but I understand why you did what you did. I would have made the same choice if it had been you in Hades. And now that I know everything, you can stay. We can be together." Something flashed behind his eyes. It looked a little like hope. "If it's still what you want."

Cautious hope.

"Hades knows the deal's been broken," Grace informed. "If you ever leave this place, he'll come for you."

Why had Hades been silent on the matter at the meeting on Olympus? Was he biding his time before he turned the knife? What was the God of the Dead was up to?

"So we'll stay here, together." Chris stood, pulling Grace up with him.

He wrapped his arms around her, burying his face in her hair. She breathed deep and for the first time in a very long time she let her guard down, let the tension bleed from every pore. She inhaled the scent of him, the sandalwood and sage and sunshine unique to Chris.

"Please, Grace. Stay with me."

Grace nuzzled into his chest, torn between mind flooding joy and bone aching wariness. She melted into him.

"I didn't kill him," Grace said, her voice muffled against his chest. "Samael, that is. I couldn't. You were right about me." She sighed, relaxing further into the curve of his body until not an inch of space separated them.

He kissed the top of her head and held her tight. "Stay," he whispered again.

It was hard to contain the sheer joy inside of her. She wanted nothing more than to curl up inside him and never let him go.

Pulling back a fraction, Grace looked up into his eyes. "Okay, but I have to go back to Olympus. For just a while."

He stroked her cheek. "Why?"

"There's stuff going on," she said. "I need to finish what I've started there. They need me, I can't just abandon them."

Chris dropped his arms and took a step back. "No. Better to

abandon me."

She grabbed his arms. "It's not like that. I'll come back as soon as I can, but I have responsibilities."

He pulled away, cutting her off and turning his back to her. "Don't you see, Grace? They won't let you come back? They want to keep us apart."

She moved in front of him, putting both hands on his chest as he held her by the arms tightly, almost too tightly. "No, please. It's not like that. I love you. I love you more than anything."

She was crying again. He slid his hands down her arms, making goose bumps break out along her skin, and clenched her by the wrists.

"Then prove it," he said. "Stay with me."

She shook her head. "I can't stay. But I promise I'll come back. Please Chris, what would you do if our positions were reversed?"

"Nothing is more important to me than you," he swore.

"You would abandon your people, your family when they needed you the most?"

Chris looked away. She knew his answer. Of course, he wouldn't. He would do whatever it took to make his family safe. Then he would return to her just as she would return to him.

"Please," Grace begged. "Just give me some time. A few weeks, that's all. I'll be back, I swear."

He walked away. Looking back over his shoulder, he offered a bitter smile. "Do what you need to. It's not like I have anywhere to go."

CHAPTER 9

Ael iacta est. [The die is cast] ~ Julius Caesar

GRACE didn't want to leave Chris that way, but there could be no happy ending today.

When I come back, she thought.

She must leave, but only to finish what needed to be done. When she returned to Aletheia, she would beg his forgiveness. Yes, she would come back and stay forever.

When Grace reached the palace, Phoenix was sitting at the round council table flanked by her advisors. Lynx stood behind her looking like some barbarian warrior. It would have been funny except for the severe frown carved into his face.

"Grace, there are things we need to discuss," Phoenix said in an official tone. She leaned forward, her garnet red butterfly wings fluttering gently.

The man next to Phoenix motioned to the chair across from them. "Please sit."

Hesitantly, Grace settled into the chair. She had never been on the receiving end of one of her aunt's stern lectures, but had the distinct feeling she was about to be.

"Grace," Phoenix said, "these are my advisers, Philip and Lucinda."

Grace nodded. "It's nice to meet you both."

They inclined their heads but remained silent.

"Grace," Phoenix began again, "I need to talk to you about what's going on in Olympus."

"All right," Grace said, shifting in her seat. Why did just sitting there feel like being in front of a firing squad? Maybe she should ask for a blindfold and a cigarette.

"What are the Greeks planning?" The woman Lucinda snapped, a feather pen perched over a blank sheet of parchment.

"Excuse me?" Grace sputtered, surprised by the aggressive tone.

Phoenix waved for Lucinda to back off. "What she means is, well, we've heard some very concerning rumors about the Olympians."

"Yes," Philip agreed. "If you could perhaps explain to us so we don't have to rely on rumor and innuendo." His voice was calm, kind even, but the hair on the back of Grace's neck stood at attention anyway.

"We've decided to reform the Council of the Gods under a new directive," Grace answered, speaking directly to Phoenix.

"To what purpose?" Phoenix asked.

Lucinda scribbled furiously.

"We just want to help people," Grace replied with a shrug. "To use what powers we have for the betterment of mankind."

Looking a bit smug, Philip sat back and folded his arms across his chest. "You realize the Olympians were specifically told they could no longer meddle in the lives of humans?"

"Yes," Grace replied. "But only because they were taking advantage, using their powers to do harm rather than good."

Philip smirked. "So you admit they are openly defying the Goddess."

Phoenix shook her head. "That's not what she said."

"The Olympians are lost," Grace said. "Drifting through their existence. Doing nothing. Being nothing. They need a purpose to unify them, to give their lives meaning."

"They had that opportunity once," Phoenix said in a gentle voice. She reached across the table and took Grace's hand. "They choose to throw it away."

Grace pulled away and slipped both hands into her lap. "They got lost. I know that. They did horrible things. I met Sybil, remember? I understand."

"When did you meet Sybil?" Phoenix asked, cocking her head to the side.

"It was before," Grace explained. She had forgotten that Phoenix had no memory of their interaction with Sybil. "You don't remember because of what Hades did."

"What is she talking about?" Lucinda demanded, looking at Phoenix.

"I'm not sure," Phoenix said, her eyebrows scrunching together.

"It happened before Hades changed everyone's memories," Grace said.

Angry, Philip bolted to his feet. "Are you saying that the Olympian God Hades has tampered with the Queen's memory?"

"Well, sort of," Grace replied. "Mnemosyne actually did the memory tampering. Not just with Phoenix, but with everyone except Lorna, me, and James. It was part of the bargain I struck with Hades."

"Guards!" Philip yelled.

Lynx stepped forward and two other guards stomped into the room.

"Seize the girl!" Phillip ordered.

"Philip!" Phoenix yelled. "What are you doing? Unhand my niece!"

"No!" Lucinda joined in. "The queen has had her mind tampered with by the Olympians. This is an act of war!"

"Majesty, we must determine the extent of the damage that has been done," Phillip said. "Faerie must be fortified! Lucinda, carry a message to the outlands. No one comes into or leaves Faerie. We must have containment, until we can determine what the reason behind this gross breach of the treaty."

"This is crazy." Grace struggled against the firm grip of the guards, who grabbed her by the arms. With them touching her, she could not blink out without taking them, too.

"Hades isn't planning some sort of takeover," Grace tried to explain. "It was me. My fault. Chris was dead and I struck a bargain to get him back."

Philip's anger spun into shocked. "My son was dead?"

Grace looked to Phoenix who sighed, rubbing her temples with her thumb and ring finger. Philip was Chris' father? Looking closely, Grace could see a resemblance.

"That is why Hades wants Chris?" Philip demanded.

"If Chris remembered," Grace answered, "the deal would be

void and his soul would go back to the Underworld."

"And you told him?" Phillip asked, his voice cracking like a whip.

"No." Grace shook her head. "Of course not. He figured it out on his own. He went to the Hall of Memory"

"Philip," Phoenix interjected. "Chris is safe as long as he remains here."

Lucinda stood and clutched her scroll to her chest. "How do we know she's not here to take Chris back to Hades?"

"This is insane!" Grace screamed, finally losing her temper.

"I'm afraid until we can straighten things out we have no choice," Phillip said. "Lock the girl in the Slithen. We must hold a full trial to determine the best course of action."

He motioned for the guards to take Grace away.

Phoenix stepped forward. "I'm not going to allow you to do this."

Phillip offered a short bow. "My Queen, your mind has been disturbed by the Greeks. We cannot know if you are somehow under their control. Whatever decision is made must be reached by the full authority of the elders."

"I have not been *disturbed*," Phoenix insisted. "I am the queen!"

"From this moment on we are relieving you of your title, pending investigation into these matters." Philip turned his back to her and snapped his fingers.

Two more guards entered the room.

Lynx tensed, ready to take on the entire palace to protect his queen.

Phoenix very calmly pulled the tall pearl crown from her head and set it on the table. She moved around Philip and walked past Grace, who was being held fast by the guards.

Grace saw Phoenix toss her a look that clearly warned not to do anything stupid, just before she exited the room with Lynx hot on her heels.

* * *

THE Slithen was nothing more than a tall hill with a door in one side. The guards tossed Grace inside and barred the round door closed behind her.

The space was tight. The floor, ceiling, and walls were made of dirt as if someone had literally just carved a pit in the side of a hill. Squeezing her eyes closed, Grace focused on Chris' room and tried to flash out. She opened her eyes to find herself still in the dark hole. She tried twice more before giving up. A familiar voice from the other side of the door surprised her.

"Grace?" a voice called through the door.

"Phoenix?"

"Yes. Are you all right?"

"I'm locked in a hole," Grace snapped. "What do you think?"

"I know. I'm so sorry. There's nothing I can do right now. They've called a trial with all the representatives from across Faerie. It will take a few days for everyone to get here."

"What do you mean a few days? And why am I going on trial?"

"It's not you going on trial, exactly. It's the Olympians." Phoenix's voice dropped to a whisper on the last part. "They've broken the treaty. Philip thinks you're a spy. If they want to, it's enough to declare war on the Greeks."

"War? That's just stupid."

"Is it? I mean, what right did Hades have to mess with everyone's memories? And most of us are old enough to remember very clearly the horrors the Olympians caused before the Goddess stepped in and put a stop to it."

"It's my fault, Phoenix. I suggested reorganizing the Olympian Council. I was the reason Hades took everyone's memories away. This is all my fault, as usual." With a sigh, Grace slid down the dirt wall and plopped onto the damp ground. "You have to talk to them. Tell them I'm the one who should be on trial. It's my doing, all of it."

"Grace, you didn't know," Phoenix said. "You couldn't have imagined."

"I know. I was trying to do the right thing. The road to hell is paved with good intentions. Isn't that how the old saying goes?"

"Grace, you can't give up. Just stay calm. I'll do what I can."

"I know you will," Grace said. "And, Phoenix?"

"Yes?"

"I'm so sorry. About what I said before. I didn't mean it, not really."

"I know. Love you."

"Love you, too."

CHAPTER 10

The God of War hates those who hesitate.
~ Euripides

"THIS is unacceptable!" Prometheus growled, slamming his fist on the arm of his throne.

The Gods who were gathered in the main temple nodded and murmured in agreement.

"How dare the Fae take an Olympian prisoner," Apollo spat.

"It's an act of war!" one shouted.

"A clear violation of the treaty," said another.

"Please." The Guardian Michael stepped forward, his shaggy brown hair falling across his forehead and shadowing his soft brown eyes. "You must remain calm. Grace is as much one of them as she is one of you."

"She's my daughter!" Prometheus protested. "My blood! How can you say she's one of them?"

"She was born in Faerie, raised by a Fae," James reminded. "You know she loves them." His eyes, one blue and one green, were bloodshot. His jeans were dirty and his black button-up shirt was wrinkled, as if he had been rolling around on the ground. His unruly hair framed a face shadowed with whiskers.

Prometheus huffed at the James. "She was stolen from me before she was even born. Then hidden away and kept from her true family by the Fae. That alone is an act of aggression. I let it pass because Grace loved them. But I'm sure after such trickery and betrayal, her loyalties have changed."

"Prometheus is right," Apollo said. "Grace is one of us. If we must, we'll bring the Fae to their knees to see her returned."

"Please." Michael raised his hand, gesturing for calm. "Allow me to speak to the Fae. I'm sure they will see the wisdom in returning Grace to Olympus."

"No," Apollo argued. "This is a slap in the face by the Fae. They must be punished!"

Michael straightened, reaching his full and impressive height. His normally dark eyes flashed gold. "I have tried to settle this with reason, but it is clear to me that you only respect force. It would server you all well to remember that I can force you, if it becomes necessary."

Prometheus stood. His long white toga flowed like water, as he walked toward Michael. "No," he said grabbing Michael's arm. "It is time the Guardians learn to respect the Olympians."

Michael moved to slap away the hand on his arm, but Prometheus caught his other hand before it made contact. They stood there, grasping each other's forearms, locked in a battle of strength and will.

Michael's mouth fell open just a fraction in surprise and Prometheus knew why. The Olympians had been stripped of their powers. Prometheus should not have been able to stand against a Guardian.

James stepped forward only to be grabbed by an equally strong Apollo, who held him tight.

Michael's shock weakened him just enough for Prometheus to push him to his knees in the center of the floor. "How?"

"The time of bowing down to the Guardians and the Fae is past," Prometheus proclaimed. "The Olympians will reclaim their glory and their power. Now go. Leave this realm. And carry a message to the Fae. Tell them the treaty is broken. They have one day to return my daughter, or it shall be war between us."

Prometheus turned his back on Michael who knelt, panting. Then he faced the Olympians.

Apollo released James and brought his clenched fist to his heart in a traditional salute. Hades rose and mimicked the action. One by one, the others followed suit before vanishing.

James helped Michael to his feet. Then they disappeared.

Prometheus smirked. It was more than a salute. It was an acknowledgement of his leadership. They had just elected him King of the Gods.

CHAPTER 11

Each of us bears his own hell.
~ Virgil

THICK smoke clung to the damp grass, rising up from the earth in hazy patches like ghosts stretching for the sky.

The sound of exploding energy blasts and the clash of metal surrounded Grace as she made her way toward the fighting. She walked blindly, unable to make out any faces. Battle raged all around her like a black and white movie. The only color was the occasional splash of brown-red blood on the ground. Bodies lay scattered. Some she knew were Fae, only because of the tattered butterfly wings that crumpled like newspaper beside them.

She paused, as her bare foot grazed something soft. Reaching down, she grabbed a handful of…what? Feathers. Raven black feathers too large to belong to any bird. She dropped them and they fluttered to the shadowy ground. Her eyes filled with tears.

Falling to her knees, she crawled in the near darkness. Her legs were wet and cold from dew. Soon her hand found something solid. Flesh. Cool flesh. Blinking she forced herself to focus. A flash of light in the distance revealed the identity she feared. It was Eros, the god of lust and her one time teacher, staring blankly into the sky. A drop of blood trickled from his nose, almost invisible on his dark skin. She pulled him into her lap, cradling his head as tears rolled down her cheeks.

How could this happen? He was supposed to be immortal! They all were!

The noise of the fighting drew closer, trapping her. She slid Eros gently to the ground and tried to stand.

There was another flash of light. She looked down at herself. It was not dew that made her white dress cling to her legs. It was blood, thick and dark.

Reaching down, she pressed her hand to the ground, bringing it she saw it was covered in blood. The ground was soggy, flooded with the blood of her friends, her family.

Lifting her head, she screamed.

* * *

GRACE fell forward in the small space, landing on her chin in the dirt. Then she remembered where she was, the Slithen.

"Ouch." She sat up, rubbing her chin.

"Grace!" Chris called from outside the Slithen. "Are you all right?"

"Yeah, I'm fine. Just a bad dream."

She pulled her knees into her chest. In the pitch darkness, Grace was not sure how much time passed, but instinctively she knew it could not have been long before Chris found her.

While she knew he could not get her out, he still loved her, and that was worth everything.

"Was it a dream or a vision?" Chris asked, his voice muffled by the Slithen.

"A vision." She didn't want to tell him about the terrible things she saw, but she refused to lie to him. If she lived a million years, she would never lie to him again.

"How bad was it?" he asked.

"It was bad," she admitted. "If anything happens to me, you have to try to talk everyone down. The Olympians and the Fae must not go to war."

"I know," Chris said. "I didn't live through the first war, but I know it was bloody enough that people still carry deep scars from it, and not just the physical kind. I think that's part of the reason everyone is so quick to jump on the idea of war."

"You'd think it would make them want to avoid it that much more," she said, digging her fingers into the soft soil at her feet.

"I think it's like a fire left to smolder." His voice carried a tone of disappointment. "The trial will start soon. I need to go and try to explain. Try to make my father understand."

Grace nodded. Then felt foolish as she remembered he could not see her through the door. "If this is something I can fix…that is, if they can just hold me responsible and leave the Olympians out of it, then so be it."

"I'm not going to let them hurt you Grace," he vowed.

She felt unworthy of such fierce loyalty and love. "Shut up and listen. If punishing me will make this better, avoid war, do it. I made a deal for you once. I trust you to make this one for me. No matter what."

He felt silent for a moment. Grace wished more than anything she could see his face.

"Quit trying to be a martyr," Chris said. "It'll be fine. Relax. I'll get this fixed."

Grace leaned back against the door and prayed he was right.

CHAPTER 12

War will never yield but to the principals of universal justice and love. ~ William Channing

PHOENIX looked around the small council room.

It was packed with dignitaries from every realm inside Faerie.

Even the demi-Fae were represented by Mimble, a tiny rainbow-winged Fae no bigger than a doorknob. It was odd that they came. The demi-Fae were usually solitary, not involving themselves in the matters of court, so it was a surprise to see Mimble in attendance.

Phoenix had traded her gown of royal gold for a simple white pantsuit. She hoped it would make her look less edgy. She needed the representatives to listen to her, to believe her, to trust her.

"Welcome everyone," Philip said. He inclined his head to the visitors, while pointedly ignoring Phoenix who sat to his left. "Thank you for arriving so quickly. You have all been made aware of the accusations against the Olympians."

"Allegations confirmed by the Greek prisoner," Lucinda chimed in. "We questioned her and she admitted the truth of these things."

Phillip glared across the table. "Yes, the Olympians have deceived us all. They've altered our memories, planted false ones. Who knows how much they've deceived us? Are we not safe from them in our own minds? Even our noble Queen has been affected."

"What say you, Queen Phoenix?" asked Ghared from the Kindor Mountains.

Short and stocky with pale skin and mica wings, Ghared was the representative from the mining clan who handled all stones and precious gems. His clan was powerful and influential. But best of all, Phoenix knew Ghared to be an honest and direct man, one she hope would not fall for the fear mongering being spread by Phillip and Lucinda.

Phoenix stood, smoothing her shirt. "Philip is correct. Philip's son Chris died fighting Lilith. Grace went to Hades and bargained for his return. Hades, the Olympian God of the Dead, and Mnemosyne, the Goddess of Memory, made a deal with Grace. The price Hades asked was Chris' memory. In order for the deal to be complete, all our memories were required to be changed as well. I agree it was, possibly a very poor decision on her part. But I believe Philip, if confronted with the loss of his son, would have done no less. Grace did it to save one of us."

The chamber fell silent, as Chris stepped forward from the back of the room and offered a formal bow. "I would like to speak on Grace's behalf," he said.

Phoenix allowed a smile.

"My son," Phillip argued, "is under the influence of not only Hades, but of the Olympian girl as well."

"Her name is Grace," Chris corrected loudly. "And she was born here in Aletheia."

"To an Olympian mother," Phillip muttered, drawing an unsympathetic glare from several members in the crowd.

"And," Chris continued, "I love her."

A whisper rolled through the room.

"You see?" Phillip tossed his hands in the air. "His judgment is jaded."

"No, it isn't," Phoenix said, her voice echoing through the hall with regal authority. "Grace loves Chris. She risked her life to get him back from Hades. She sacrificed her own happiness to bring him home to us. She left Faerie in order to protect him, to insure he could live out his life in peace."

"She put us all in Hades' power," Philip protested.

"Hades didn't want to control us," Phoenix countered, trying to remain calm as she clenched her hands behind her back so hard her fingernails bit into her palms. "He only wanted Grace to suffer. That was the true price of her bargain, Chris' life for her pain. The memory alterations were only a side effect."

Ghared knotted his fingers under his bearded chin. "I would

have done the same to save one of my own. It seems to me that she is guilty of bad judgment only."

"But, good sir, that is not all," Phillip added. "The girl has also admitted to leading the Olympians to unite, to reform the council the Mother herself disbanded."

Phoenix wanted nothing more than to reach over and slap Philip at that moment.

"If they are allowed to do this, the mortal world will once more be at their mercy," Lucinda said.

"Do you deny these claims?" Ghared asked Phoenix.

She shook her head. "No. Grace says they wish only to help the humans, to find a noble purpose in their existence."

Phillip glared at Phoenix. "We've all seen how that ends."

What could she say to that? They were right. The Olympians had never been trustworthy. Grace's desire for family left her blind to their faults, to their history of cruelty and selfishness.

"I agree that it cannot be allowed," Ghared said. "Perhaps we should seek the guidance and assistance of the Guardians."

From the back of the room, the Guardian Michael stepped forward. "We've gone to speak to the Olympians already. I'm afraid we bring troubling news. Not only do they see Grace's imprisonment as a violation of the treaty, they say you have one day to return her to Olympus or they will declare war."

"Let them come," Philip said with an air of dismissal. "They are practically powerless. We would crush them."

Michael frowned, moving forward to the center of the meeting with James following behind him.

"That is no longer accurate," Michael said. Then he explained what they had witnessed in the Temple of All the Gods.

* * *

JAMES had no desire to listen to the Fae bicker.

When no one was looking, he vanished from the council chamber and reappeared outside the Slithen where Grace was being held.

The last time they had seen each other was when she refused his offer to join the Guardians. Now, being short one Guardian, they were busier than ever. James threw himself back into his duties with gusto. Rejection, it was his first, left an unpleasant and painful sting. He always got what he wanted, even as a human. Not without hard work, but eventually. Now he was wandering around Faerie, twisted in knots over some girl. Magnificent girl though she was.

Grace was not like other women he had known. She was an odd combination of bold and reckless, kind and stubborn. Half the time he wanted to throttle her. She was always so determined to do the right thing for everyone that she kept putting herself in harm's way. Selfless to the point of near stupidity. Yet when she had stood against Lilith, James saw in her a determination of will glazed with a rage so powerful he was sure she could have brought the world crashing to its knees if she desired it. She was a warrior in spirit, the perfect match to his own. She risked her life to save his and in doing so put the entire world in jeopardy. Yet she defended the decision, as if somehow, she thought he was worth the risk.

It made his heart swell that she thought so much of him.

Yet she persisted in chasing after Christopher Le Fae as if her existence depended on his faerie whims. It was pathetic.

Now she had left the safety of Olympus and landed herself in another mess that James would have to clean up. It didn't upset him as much as he thought it would. To be honest, some small part of him relished the fact that he would be the one to rush in and rescue her yet again. Eventually she would stop chasing the impossible and would look at him, instead. She would see that they belonged together.

There were no guards at the Slithen. Of course, none was necessary. The Slithen was the one place from which no one could escape. The magic that held Grace in prison was ancient, more than a match for God or Fae.

The hill itself was grassy, sloping with a dark round wooden door carved into the base. There was no knob or lock. It was the magic that held it closed and only magic could open it.

"Grace?" James called, leaning against the door.

"James, is that you?"

"Yeah, I'm here. How are you holding up?"

"Are you kidding me with that?" Grace gave a dry laugh.

"Point taken."

James knew Grace was never one to surrender. He suspected she would wag her sharp tongue into the fires of hell.

"Listen," he said through the door, "the Fae are losing their minds out here. The Olympians too. Prometheus challenged Michael, Grace. And he won."

"What does that mean?"

"It means your father is at full strength again. Do you have any idea how that might have happened?"

"No. I swear. I had no idea."

James sighed, pressing the palms of his hands against the door and giving it a futile push. "I believe you. But with everything going on, I don't know how we can avoid this turning into a full blown fight."

"James, you can't let that happen," Grace said urgently.

He could almost feel her on the other side of the door, her hands mirroring his own. Her voice shook just enough to tell him she was truly afraid, not for herself—never for herself, but for everyone else. As usual.

"I don't know what I can do," James said giving the door a pound with balled fists. He needed to get her out of the Slithen. The must be a way. He was a Guardian, for Goddess' sake.

He sat outside the door, trying to come up with a plan. Then something dawned on him. Grace was powerful enough to create an earthquake. It was not something she could just call upon, but there might be a way. He rolled to his feet and pressed his forehead against the door.

"We need to get you out of there," James declared.

"How? I can't flash out. Every time I try, I bounce off like a bird flying into a window. The door won't budge. Besides, if they find out you helped me, who knows what they will do to you?"

There she goes again, he thought. Always worried about everything but her own preservation. He hoped he could count on that trait for the next few minutes.

"You mean like declare war on the Olympians?" he asked,

baiting her. "I'm afraid that ship has sailed. At least if we get you home, it might cool down your father at bit. He's not thinking rationally. None of them are."

James stepped back, steeling himself for what he had decided to do next. If there was any doubt in his mind, the exhaustion and frustration in her voice ate it away.

"That still doesn't explain how I'm gonna bust out of here," Grace said.

"You aren't going to like it," James whispered barely loud enough for her to hear.

"At this point, I'll try anything," she responded.

He sighed, knowing this would be the one exception to that statement. "You're going to have to call the Roth De Shar."

"No way!" Grace roared.

He had expected as much. The Roth De Shar was dangerous, and James understood her fear. It was a very rare ability that allowed a person to kill with just the sound of their voice. Unfortunately, it fills the user with an uncontrollable rage. She had said it felt like maggots crawling under her skin. To use it, she must allow herself to be taken over by hatred. She used it one time, when she thought Chris was dead. The rage and grief had been almost too much for her to handle.

"Forget it," Grace argued. "No way. I'd rather just stay here."

He growled. Why did she have to be so difficult? "And let your family fight, probably die?"

She was quiet.

A string of obscenities let loose in his head. He wanted to tell her how stupid she was being. He wanted to shake some sense into her. But he knew from experience that neither of those things worked. There was only one chink in Grace's armor. And James knew exactly what it was.

"It might be the only way to get you out," he said gently, trying to persuade her to reason.

"I don't care," she said.

Stupid, stubborn, pigheaded girl.

James pounded the door with both fists. "Grace, please. If we don't get you home, your father and the Olympians are going to start a war. And it will be your fault."

Silence.

"Please," James begged.

"What do I need to do?" Grace asked finally.

James was not sure how her power would affect the magic of the Slithen, but they had to try. "Focus your energy on the door. I'll do what I can from this side. Put your hands on the door."

"Okay, now what?" she asked.

He closed his eyes and concentrated on pushing his powers into the door.

"It's like when you're healing someone," James said. "Try to channel the energy into your hands and then push that energy into the door. We're going to try to overload its circuit, in a way. Understand?"

"I think so. But James?"

"Yeah?"

"I don't know if I can do this."

"Grace, you're the strongest person I've ever met. And I don't just mean your power. You have strength inside you that, to be honest, amazes me. I know you can do this. We'll do it together."

James felt her rage through the door. He pushed more energy into the door and felt the wood start to buckle along with his knees.

"James, you have to stop!" she called.

He ignored her.

"James! Stop!"

He felt the Slithen draining him. If he continued, he knew it would strip his powers completely and permanently. Once upon a time Grace had been willing to sacrifice herself to save him. Now he was counting on it.

He used to believe her compassion was a sign of weakness, but now he knew better. Compassion, not rage, was her strength. Her greatest power. He just hoped she would figure that out before it was too late.

CHAPTER 13

Darkness cannot drive out darkness; only light can do that. Hate cannot drive out hate; only love can do that. ~ Martin Luther King Jr.

GRACE threw herself against the door, shoulder first as she had seen done so many times on television. All she managed to do was hurt herself.

Trying another tactic, she clawed at the wood like a trapped animal. James was out there and he was dying. She could feel it.

Tears slid down her face.

She loved James, not the way she loved Chris, but it was there nonetheless. Grace didn't know when it happened, but James was one of the few people in her life that she would fight to defend. To kill for. To die for. He was her family in every way that mattered. He may irritate her most of the time and she was sure the feeling was mutual, but she refused to let him die trying to save her.

Stupid, stubborn, irritating Guardian.

A sleeping giant awakened inside her, exploding from every pore of her body. The blistering heat on her skin was intense and painful. Biting her bottom lip, she accepted the pain. It felt similar to the Roth De Shar, but this was more like someone else taking over her body.

Grace then realized that *she* was the power. They were one and the same, and she could control it.

She laughed, as the pain subsided. She felt like a second sun floating in the sky, burning with energy and light.

And sure enough, as she blinked, the Slithen filled with golden light, illuminating the dirt walls. She could now see the roots from trees above in the mound, hanging down into the room like macabre arms.

Turning her attention to the door, she laid one hand on it and pushed, not with her arm but with the power.

For a moment she could see beyond the door, as if it were made of thin paper.

On the other side James flew back, landing in the dirt. He lay there panting with exhaustion.

Grace reached out again and pushed. This time the door exploded out, splinters of wood falling from the sky like rain.

* * *

JAMES had been afraid she would not figure it out in time, afraid the magic would drag him under completely.

But just when he almost gave up hope, he saw Grace through the door, glowing like a star in the sky. For a brief second he wanted to cry out with joy. Then he had been flying through the air, the door blasted outward.

He blinked once, then again, before reaching up to touch her face.

"You are so beautiful," he breathed, as she pulled him to his feet.

"No, I look like a lightning bug," Grace said, crinkling her nose. Her glow was already beginning to fade.

Before either of them could say anything else, a horn sounded and the Fae came running.

The first to arrive was Lynx, who stopped short of the Slithen, dazed by what he saw.

James knew exactly why he was reacting that way. Grace stood in the dim evening light, glowing like a star fallen from the heavens. She was a Goddess. It was hard not to stare.

It was not long before they were surrounded by others. Phoenix and Chris pushed past the awed masses and into the front.

James took a step to the side, waiting for Grace to run into Chris' arms, but she didn't.

Grace stood with her hands folded in front of her.

Chris' mouth fell open at the sight of her. James understood the reaction.

She still glowed, though less bright now. It was still more

than enough to give everyone who saw her pause.

"Grace," Chris said. He took a step forward, but his father grabbed his arm and held him fast. Chris shook the hand from his arm, never looking at his father.

"The Olympians are preparing to declare war on the Fae," Grace said. Although her voice never rose above a whisper, it carried across the field as though she were using a microphone. "I will not allow that to happen. I'm sorry for any wrongs I have done you, but they were my crimes and mine alone. After I have an opportunity to speak to the Olympians, I will return and allow you to pass whatever judgment on me you think I deserve. But I will not allow you or them to be hurt anymore because of my mistakes, Chris." Her voice broke as she said his name. "I'm so sorry, for everything. I will speak to Mnemosyne and have your memories restored. But I cannot control Hades. If you leave this place, you will die. I wish things could be different." She took a step toward him and lowered her head, speaking only to him, a look of pure love on her face. "When I come back, I'll stay here with you, if that's what you want. I'd stay with you forever."

James finally understood. She would never look at him in such a way.

Grace loved James. He could feel it. But it was a pale shadow of what she felt for Chris and always would be.

The realization should have hurt, but it didn't. As much as James loved Grace, he didn't look at her that way either. He just felt surprised.

Grace turned to James and held out her hand to him. The glow of her skin was very soft now, but still beautiful.

James smiled, tension melting off him in buckets. He looked to Chris, who was still being restrained by his father, and offered a smile he hoped conveyed understanding.

Their battle was over.

James took Grace's hand and they vanished.

CHAPTER 14

*There are strings in the human heart that had
better not be vibrated.* ~ Charles Dickens

GRACE arrived with James on the outskirts of Olympus.

Stepping into the legendary realm, she knew immediately that something was wrong.

She called out to any Gods who would hear. Only one appeared.

"Hermes, what's happened?" Grace asked, waving her hand at the barren streets and empty temples.

Once musical fountains were silent and bone dry. The eyes of the statues remained closed with no magic to animate them.

"The Olympians have left," Hermes explained. "To plan an attack on the Fae." His usual surfer boy style had been replaced by a loose military black pants tied over matching boots. His shirt looked like the same material used for bullet-proof vests, but black and silver with intricately embroidered Greek letters.

"What do you mean?" James asked. "They can't attack the Fae. They can't get into Faerie."

Hermes blinked and a long handled hammer appeared in his hand. "The plan is to go to the Gateways. If Grace isn't returned by sundown, they will destroy the gates. Not just the Goat Island gateway." Hermes leveled a stern look at Grace. "There are Gods at every gate. Apollo believes if we destroy the gates, the Fae will be trapped, unable to ever get out."

Grace shook her head. "But I'm here. I'm out. We have to stop them. How long 'til sundown?"

"A few hours," James replied. "Ten minutes here, give or take."

Grace remembered the time difference between Olympus and the mortal world.

"Prometheus is on his way to the Goat Island gate," Hermes said. He paused, giving a deep frown. "He was going to Hephaestus' forge first. To get some silver swords. If any Fae manage to escape, he will cut them down."

Grace could not believe it. Silver was toxic to Fae. That her father could be so ruthless, so cold, made her heart hurt.

"That doesn't make any sense," James interjected. "He doesn't know Grace escaped. If he destroys the gates, as far as he knows, he'd be trapping Grace inside as well."

Hermes leveled his eyes on the Guardian. "Prometheus is allowing his rage to cloud his judgment. This is no longer about Grace. It is about having a convenient excuse to do what he has wanted to do for a very long time. End the Fae."

"If he's off his rocker, then why are the other Gods listening to him?" Grace asked.

"I don't know," Hermes admitted. "But Prometheus has regained almost all of his former powers. If we don't give him our loyalty, he could choose to destroy us."

"My father would never do something like that," Grace argued. In truth, she didn't really know her father that well. She wanted to believe he was a good man, but was he?

"Perhaps not. But power corrupts even the noblest of men. We lived under the rule of a nearly mad Zeus long enough to fear those powers. I'm sorry, Grace. The war is beginning. You need to choose a side." Hermes turned to James. "And you should know that Michael and Baal are in Faerie as well. They've chosen sides in this battle. Prometheus has declared them traitors. All of the Guardians."

James nodded.

Sliding a silver helmet on his head, Hermes vanished.

Grace put a hand on James arm. "Warn the Fae," she said. "I'm going to get my bow and try to meet my father at the gateway. I have to try to talk him down."

James nodded.

"And, James, thanks," Grace added, before he could disappear as well. "I know what you did back there for me."

She leaned forward and put a kiss on his cheek, leaving James looking a bit dumbfounded. Part of her expected him to react, to declare his love again. She instantly regretted the kiss.

James just offered a relaxed smile and gave her a mock salute before vanishing.

Grace smiled to herself as she realized what his reaction meant. Basically, they were good. Best of all, they were friends.

* * *

IN a blink Grace was in her temple. Pulling her bow from where she had left it under her bed, a familiar voice startled her.

"I see you made it out safely," Prometheus said.

Grace stood, expelling a relieved breath. "Yeah, I'm fine. You can call off the troops."

He motioned for her to sit beside him on the foot of her bed.

She complied, holding her bow and quiver on her lap. She tried not to show the tension she was feeling. Had he actually been looking for a reason to start a war with the Fae? When he looked at her that way, with the eyes of a loving parent, it was hard to remember why she was so suspicious of him. It was hard to remember anything.

"I will speak to Apollo and try to smooth things over with the Fae," he stated, his face tight. "You look like you are about to fall over."

Grace exhaled, suddenly overwhelmed with exhaustion. He was right. She had expelled so much power she was running on pure adrenaline. Now it hit her like a ton of bricks. She fought to keep her eyelids open.

Slumping against him for support, she succumbed to a huge yawn. "Tired. I used my powers to get out of the Slithen."

Prometheus was tense, as he laid her back on the bed. "The Slithen? How did you get out?"

Grace mumbled, but was too tired to form coherent words.

Prometheus stroked her hair. "It's all right Grace. I'm going to take care of everything," he soothed.

Grace managed a smile before slipping into a deep slumber.

* * *

"GRACE?" Prometheus asked.

She didn't respond. Her chest rose and fell slowly from the deep sleep into which he had placed her.

He withdrew the Eye of Hera from the sleeve of his shirt. Pressing the orb against Grace's forehead, he drew her powers into it.

When he was finished and the orb once more glowed with pulsating golden light, he laid a hand over her eyes and conjured an image.

* * *

GRACE knew where she was now. It was Goat Island.

The unmistakable ruins of the old fort overgrown with shades of green moss surrounded her. The fog was dense, the sky dim, the scent of sulfur thick in the air as sounds of battle enveloped her while she stood on the edge of the old cistern, looking into the still murky water.

For a second, she thought it might be a memory of the first battle with Lilith. Chris' voice called out behind her. She turned slowly this time, not wanting to be tricked again.

But it was not a memory. Behind her, Chris was thrown through the air and slammed into a tree so hard green leaves fell from the sky like rain from the impact. He bounced off the thick trunk with a bone crunching sound and fell face first into the thick carpet of ferns below.

"No," a deep male voice called over the commotion. "He's mine."

Hades strode past Eris who had been fighting Chris. She snorted, flung her black pigtails over her shoulders and danced off to fight someone else.

Hades looked more frightening than Grace remembered in his battle gear which consisted of flat black armor from head to toe. There was no shine to it, and it allowed him to be all but invisible in the shadows. The only color was the strip of his face left exposed from his chin to his eyebrows, and a Mohawk of red feathers that sprouted from his helmet.

Grace found herself immobilized. Frozen in place, not by her own fear but by some unseen force. She watched as, for the second time, Chris was consumed by the fog and vanished. She knew he was being carried back to the Underworld. Even her vocal chords were paralyzed, stifling the screams inside her head.

In a blur of motion, Phoenix rushed at Hades, swinging a halberd as she moved. She caught him off guard as he turned to look at her and sliced through the face hole in his armor. A spray of blood exploded, leaving a garish pattern on the trees and across the front of Phoenix's white leather corset and pants.

A flash of light from behind sent Phoenix falling forward, onto the unmoving body of Hades. The back of her outfit was scorched black, exposing a large wound between her shoulder blades.

Prometheus stepped out of the forest, a glowing energy ball in his hand. Before he could use it to finish off Phoenix, he was attacked from both sides by armed Fae that Grace didn't recognize. They struggled in a violent dance that moved so fast Grace could not keep up with it. There were screams all around her and the sound of bodies hitting the ground.

Slowly, in obvious pain, Phoenix struggled to her feet. From a leather pouch hanging at her side, she retrieved the Eye of Hera. She moved like a cat, crouching along the ground, and came up behind Prometheus. Reaching out, she knocked him off his feet and pounced on his back, holding the orb to the back of his head as he screamed.

The scene faded to white. Grace hugged herself, bracing for a cold that never came. In the nothingness a clear female voice rang out, sending tremors through Grace's body.

"Come to me," the voice commanded.

Taking an involuntary step forward, Grace reached out to the voice and tumbled forward into the white expanse.

* * *

PROMETHEUS stepped out of Grace's temple and called to his most loyal general.

"Apollo, I have a gift for you."

Apollo appeared dressed in shining gold armor with his bow,

much like the one he had given Grace, slung across his back.

Prometheus held out the glowing orb. "Here. Share this among the Gods who are fighting with us. It is time we put an end to the Fae, once and for all."

CHAPTER 15

*The flame keeps gnawing into her tender marrow hour by hour
and deep in her heart the silent wound lives on.* ~ Virgil

JAMES never made it to Faerie.

There were Gods at every gate he knew of, and a shocking amount of them had somehow regained their full powers. One on one, it would be a fight. Three on one, it would be suicide.

With a frustrated huff, he closed his eyes and focused on Grace. Maybe he could catch up with her, and they could put an end to the siege before it went any further. He didn't hold out much hope that she could talk the Olympians out of a full-blown conflict. But if anyone had a chance, it was Grace.

James frowned, concentrating harder, his brows pulling together over the bridge of his nose. His eyes flew open. There was nothing. He could not feel her anywhere. A split second of worry gave way to irritation.

What had the girl gotten into now?

He flashed back to Olympus, deciding to pick up her trail from there.

Following the lingering resonance of her unique energy, he stepped into her temple. He pushed back the sheer curtain that lead to her bedchamber.

She was sprawled across the white linen, sweat clinging to her entire body. Her face was twisted in pain and a soft, constant whimpering escaped her pale lips.

In a panic, James rushed to her. He brushed the wet hair from her face.

"Grace!" He shook her gently at first and then harder, until her head lolled back and forth. "Grace, wake up!"

Her eyes didn't open. Her flesh was clammy, waxy, and dull.

Laying her back down, James rushed to her bathroom and

headed straight for her bathtub. He turned on the faucet for cold water. The tub was not actually connected to any water lines or drains. It was only there the temple because Grace wanted it.

The tub filled quickly with ice-cold water. James turned off the faucet and hurried back to the bed.

Effortlessly, he lifted Grace and carried her to the bath.

"Sorry about this," he mumbled, feeling a smile tug at his lips. He had wanted to do something like this to her since the moment they had met.

More carefully than in his irritated daydreams, James lowered Grace into the icy water. She slid in, only his grip keeping her head above the water line. There was a grunt, but otherwise she remained still.

Scooping up handfuls of water, he splashed her face. If she felt anything, he could not tell.

"Grace, you must wake up." He slapped her face. "Grace!"

No response.

He rocked back on the balls of his feet and wiped a hand across his forehead. As soon as he let go of her, she slid under the surface of the water. He reached down and pulled her face back out, slumping her over the edge of the tub.

Then, he had a thought.

Most of the Gods were equipped with an internal survival trigger. Even if they were inches from death, their bodies would automatically fight for life.

He pulled her away from the edge of the tub and held her head above the water. It was a risk. In her condition she could just as easily slip away. James bit his lip.

"Forgive me," he muttered, as he pushed her under the water.

She was immortal, after all. She would not actually drown. Still, he was not comfortable seeing her under the water.

Small bubbles escaped her nose and mouth. Her eyes remained closed. Her mouth opened beneath the surface. Then her body began to buck, sending water sloshing over the edges.

Every fiber in his body wanted to reach down and snatch her out of the tub, but he knew he must wait.

One second. Two seconds. Four seconds.

She went still beneath the water. Bubbles rose faster and bigger, as the last bits of precious oxygen leaked from her body.

Swearing, James reached in to pull her out. He snatched his hand back quickly. It was not air causing the bubbles. The water turned from ice cold to boiling. He attempted to reach in again and cried out from the pain.

The bubbles completely obscured Grace.

He cradled his hand to his chest, as the blisters healed and the redness faded.

Water splashed over the side again. But it was too much. More water than the tub could possible hold ran like a stream onto the stone floor. James tried to stand, but slipped and fell backwards. Before he could try again, the heavy porcelain tub exploded, sending shards flying through the air and scraping across the floor.

Grace rolled out onto the ground, water leaking from the corners of her mouth before she settled back into slow, even breathing.

"Well, that didn't go as hoped," James grumbled, as he crawled forward on his knees. Now they were both soaked.

He put a hand on her face. She had gone from cold and clammy to feverish.

Scooping her up, James carried her back to the bed and laid her on it.

What was he going to do now? He was not a healer. He could not count on the Olympians. In fact, one of them must have done this to her.

But who would want to....

The question died on his lips.

Prometheus. That was how he and other Olympians had regained their powers. They were draining Grace of her energy, using her like a walking battery.

Rage boiled inside him. If he could get his hands on Prometheus, he would squeeze the life out of him and watch the light bleed from his eyes. Never in all his life had he wanted to kill anyone so badly. And he had lived a very, very long time.

James sat on the bed, his hands digging into the fine silk

blankets. He must find a way to get to Faerie and try to head off the coming war.

Slumping over, James cracked his knuckles. The immediate relief of pressure felt good. It was a habit from long ago, one he worked hard to break, a physical manifestation of his fears. He hadn't resorted to it for years, centuries perhaps. Not since his human life at the river Beas, when his army turned had against him in revolt.

He had never felt so alone, so powerless.

CHAPTER 16

*So it is that the gods do not give
all men gifts of grace.* ~ Homer

WOODSTOCK, Virginia was both isolated and beautiful.

It was the third and last gateway to Faerie in the United States, the first being in Washington and the second in North Carolina. The entrance was well hidden in the dense woods, but still rarely used. A fire watchtower had been erected. It was a popular spot for visitors and, unfortunately, gave a very good view of the civil war ruins that surrounded the gateway two miles to the west.

As James closed in carefully, stepping through the thick underbrush, he knew he was in the right place. Standing back-to-back only feet apart were Hermes and Eros. Eros was a solitary creature, much like James, but they were both fond of Grace. James just hoped it would be enough.

"James." Hermes held out his hand.

James stepped into the clearing and over a pile of rubble that once had been part of a Confederate outpost. Taking Hermes hand, he patted the Olympian on the back.

"I'm glad I found you," James said. "There's a problem. It's Grace."

"What happened?" Hermes asked. "Is she all right?"

Eros stepped closer, listening. His hand tensed on his black long bow.

"No," James answered. "She's unconscious. She might be dying."

Eros snorted. "How is such a thing possible?"

"I suspect that someone, one of the Olympians, has been using the Eye of Hera to drain her powers," James explained.

"Prometheus," Hermes spat.

James splayed his fingers. "I don't have any proof."

"It would explain too much to be a falsehood," Eros said thoughtfully.

"Prometheus is too powerful for us to challenge openly. And if he does have the Eye of Hera...." Hermes paused, looking around. "Still, we can't leave."

James expected that response. Still, it disappointed him.

"I may know a way to save Grace, but I'll need help," James said. "Eros, I just need you to look the other way."

Eros' eye twitched. "My father was the God of War. If there's to be a battle, I would be a great asset."

"Thank you, Eros. I hope it doesn't come to that," James said, feeling better knowing he was on their side.

"What do you need from me?" Hermes asked.

"Nothing yet," James said. "I'm going into Faerie. You just stay here and wait for my word. You are the cavalry. When I call, you come running, okay?"

"Prometheus has ordered us to destroy the gateway at sundown," Eros informed. "You have less than an hour."

"It'll be enough," James said with more confidence than he felt.

Hermes jerked his head. Then both he and Eros turned their backs to James and the small well that served as the gateway.

James kicked away the loose boards that covered the top and jumped into the well.

Thankfully, as a Guardian James didn't need an invitation to enter either realm. He flashed from the field just beyond the Fae capital city of Aletheia to outside the room of the one person who might be able to save Grace.

Standing in front of the thick wooden door, James balled his hands into fists. On any other day he might be knocking on this door to instigate a fight. Today he was going to have to swallow his pride and ask for help.

Raising his arm, James forcefully rapped twice.

The door swung open, and James stared into the eyes of the one person he hated the most, Christopher Le Fae.

Chris leaned out the door, looking down both sides of the

hallway. "Is Grace with you?" he whispered.

"Why, you want to throw her in prison again?" James asked, folding his arms across his chest.

Chris' jaw ticked as he stepped back. "What do you want?" he demanded.

James dropped his arms and tried to be civil. "I didn't come here to fight. I suppose old habits die hard. We need to talk. Can I come in?"

Chris narrowed his eyes, but stepped back. After James entered, he closed the door behind them.

"It's Grace," James said. "She's in trouble."

Chris raked his fingers through his hair. "What else is new?" he asked with a tired, sarcastic laugh.

"I believe that the Olympians are using her," James said.

"You mean using her as an excuse to pick a fight with the Fae. Yeah, I figured. Of course, the Fae are using her to pick a fight with the Olympians." Chris shrugged.

James stepped forward, barely resisting the urge to punch the boy. *What does she see in this pathetic creature?*

"No. Someone has been draining her powers. She's weak. Very weak. Unconscious. I can't get her to wake up."

Chris sat on the edge of his bed, holding his head in his hands. "I don't know what I can do."

"All this, it's gone too far. I'm afraid Grace might be the only one strong enough to stop it."

Chris looked up, his face resigned. "I agree, but what do you expect me to do about it? Fairy tales aside, she isn't sleeping beauty, and I'm certainly not prince charming."

James snorted in agreement, earning him a sharp look.

"I believe I've discovered how to get Grace to tap into her powers," James said.

Chris' head snapped up. "No. I won't help you force her to call on the Roth De Shar. The rage is poison to her."

"No. I admit, for a while I believed it was her anger that fueled her, but it's not. It's something much more frightening. It's love."

Chris looked confused. "What do you mean?"

"She called on the Roth De Shar, not in anger or grief but in love, love for you. And in the end, it was that love that called her back to herself. It was her love that healed me and Eris. It was her love that allowed her to break herself free of the Slithen. Don't you see? All this time I had it wrong. It wasn't the darkness inside herself she needed to embrace. It was the light. And you, better than anyone, bring out the light in her."

"Say you're right. That still leaves the question of what I'm supposed to do about it. I'm stuck here, remember?"

James nodded, waiting for Chris to catch on. "Yes. If you leave, Hades will take you back to the Underworld. I was there when the deal was struck. But I'm thinking she needs something to shock her back into some kind of awareness to force her to tap into those powers."

Chris stared for a minute and then the light seemed to click on in his brain. "You want me to sacrifice myself to Hades in hopes of shocking Grace awake."

James nodded. "If I could do it myself, believe me I would. Losing you again is going to destroy her. You understand that? But the other option is no option at all."

How could Grace love such a coward? She had risked her life for Chris more than once and this was how he was going to repay her? He was not worthy of her anyway. All these things sprang to his mind in a heartbeat.

"How do we do this?" Chris asked, standing up.

James was surprised. Almost impressed. "Once we get to past the Woodstock gate, we'll flash to Olympus where Hermes will invite you inside. Hopefully, we can get to Grace before Hades senses you and tracks us down."

"And then?" Chris asked.

"And then you die, again." James gave a casual shrug. "The rest is up to Grace."

Chris rolled his eyes. "Well, that sounds like a great plan."

"You got a better one?" James hissed.

"Nope," Chris said, rubbing his chin. "So let's get going. I was getting bored sitting around here anyway."

CHAPTER 17

*Our greatest pretenses are built up not to hide the evil
and ugly in us, but our emptiness.* ~ Eric Hoffer

EROS rolled his eyes skyward and Hermes slapped himself in the forehead the moment James and Chris appeared on the other side of the gateway.

"You two are idiots," Hermes growled.

"Quick!" James said, putting a hand on the Hermes' shoulder. "Go to Olympus and invite Chris in."

"Oh, no," Eros said with a smirk, "I'm not missing this one."

Then four of them vanished together.

* * *

HERMES stood beside Grace's limp body.

Around her neck was a jewel he remembered. It was a tear shaped sapphire, the same kind Prometheus once gave to Pandora. Hermes wrapped his hand around the stone and pulled. The chain snapped. He tossed it over his shoulder and it skidded across the floor into the far wall.

"Christopher!" he yelled, calling the Fae into Olympus.

In a flash of light there were three men standing around the bed. Another flash and they were four.

"We don't have much time," Hermes warned. "I can feel Hades. He's coming."

"Grace, can you hear me?" Chris asked, rushing to the bed. He leaned over and brushed a kiss over her lips. "We need you to wake up. I need you to wake up."

"It looks like you were right about one thing," James said.

Chris shot him a questioning look.

"You are definitely no prince charming," James added.

Just as Chris opened his mouth to say something, Hades

appeared in the room.

His black battle armor added unneeded inches all the way around his the muscular form. With his helmet tucked under his arm, Hades walked closer to the group.

Eros twitched, as if prepared to put himself between Hades and Chris. But Chris gave a subtle shake of the head, and Eros froze where he stood.

"What do we have here?" Hades asked, glaring at the small group. "Hermes, Eros, don't you have somewhere else you're supposed to be?"

"Grace is ill, Hades," Hermes said, unfazed by Hades not-so-subtle threat. "I'm sure Prometheus won't begrudge us leaving to tend to his daughter."

"And you, Fae. Are you here to tend to Grace, as well?" Hades gave a short, deep laugh. "Better do it quickly. I'm afraid your time in this world is up."

"Hades, will she die?" Hermes asked.

Hades moved forward to the edge of the bed and laid a hand on her head, making Chris and James twitch nervously.

"No," he answered with a dismissive wave of his hand. "She is immortal still. She will linger like this."

"For how long?" Chris asked.

"I do not know," Hades answered with a shrug. "I suspect until she recovers strength enough to wake herself. Hours, days, eons. It's impossible to tell."

Chris stroked her chin. "Grace, please. You have to wake up. Come on, I know you can hear me."

Hades cleared his throat. "Touching, really. But, I am on a bit of a schedule, so let's get on with this." Hades reached out to Chris. "Take my hand please."

Chris went rigid at Grace's side.

"This can be pleasant, or not," Hades reminded.

Chris leaned over Grace's still body and kissed her forehead. "Goodbye, Grace. I love you."

Then Chris took Hades' outstretched hand.

CHAPTER 18

*Absence lessens the minor passions and increases the great
ones, as the wind douses a candle and kindles a fire.*
~ Francois La Rochefoucauld

GRACE had never been so alone, or so lost.

An eternal darkness stretched out around her. There was no noise other than the occasional disembodied voice whispering to her. No scents. No sensation of any kind. Just emptiness. She felt hollow, like a seashell. If someone were to hold her to their ear, would they hear the ocean inside her?

She hurt everywhere, as if every muscle in her body had strained to the breaking point. Her mouth was dry and her lips cracked.

A tear slid down her cheek. By the time she reached up to catch it, it was gone. Nothing but a memory.

"Come," the voice whispered again.

She ignored it. There was nothing attached to it. It was just some delusion torturing her.

She tried to escape. She ran, and then walked until her legs and arms burned with the effort. In her blindness, she could have been running in circles.

Finally, her strength gone, she fell to her knees. Even that hurt, so she lay down and curled onto her side with her eyes squeezed closed against the relentless darkness.

"Grace, can you hear me?" Chris' voice echoed in the darkness. "We need you to wake up. I need you to wake up."

His was a new voice. Was it another trick, her cruel mind punishing her for leaving him behind?

There in the darkness, everything finally became clear. She should never have left Chris. He needed her and she needed him. They were more together than each was alone. She should have found another way to stop the violence. Once again, she had rushed into what she thought was right and had ended up making things worse.

"Chris?" she called hoarsely, her throat burning. "Where are you?"

Silence.

Then from the darkness, a dim light grew until it framed the body of a woman. She was so beautiful, so familiar.

"Persephone?"

Persephone nodded, her long golden hair flowing around her in waves, lifted by a breeze Grace could neither hear nor feel.

"Grace, you look like hell, no pun intended."

"Where am I?" Grace managed weakly as she sat forward, holding herself up on trembling arms.

"You're in the Underworld, of course." Persephone's lovely face donned a frown. "Well, to be completely accurate, you're in the Netherworld."

"The Netherworld?" Grace asked, clearing her parched throat with a cough that did more harm than good. The salty copper taste of blood filled Grace's mouth.

Persephone smiled. "Yes, the place between life and death. Neither here, nor there. The Netherworld."

It seemed wrong to sit at Persephone's feet, but Grace would never be able to hold herself up on her own. It was better to sit that than fall on her face, she supposed.

"Why am I here? And why are you here?"

"You, my dear, are lingering here. I have come to lead you back."

Grace shook her head and pain shot her between the eyes. For a moment she was afraid she would black out. She squeezed her eyes shut and took a few deep breaths. Then she opened one eye experimentally. "I don't understand."

Persephone lifted the hem of her forest green toga and knelt beside Grace. "Your powers have been drained, nearly to the point of death. Eventually, you could heal yourself, but I'm afraid I just can't wait that long."

"Wait for what?" Grace asked, pain dulling her senses.

Persephone rolled her eyes. "For you, child. The Gods are at war, remember?"

"Yes, thanks for reminding me. I forgot." Grace stretched her back. "What's the big deal for you, though? I mean, it's not like the Fae can kill the Gods. It's the Fae who will be hurt."

"That is not entirely accurate," Persephone replied. "The Fae have fought the Gods once before. They are well aware of our weaknesses. And now they have the support of the Guardians. I assure you, if this battle happens, it will be a bloodbath."

"Wait," Grace said. "So what happens if Hades is killed? Do people just stop dying?"

A look of sheer terror shot across Persephone's face. The idea of losing her husband was the one thing that could damage her renowned calm.

"Of course not." Persephone's jaw was tight. Her fierce eyes glowed gold. "Another would be chosen to take his place. But I would be without a husband, and I have no intention of letting that happen." She gave a conspiratorial smile. "Luckily, I have you, and you can put an end to this madness. That is, if we can get you out of here."

Chris' voice echoed through the darkness again.

"Goodbye, Grace," it whispered. "I love you."

The last the cobwebs in Grace's mind cleared enough to let her know she was not imagining his voice. Chris was somewhere close, and he was calling out to her.

Grace grabbed the folds of Persephone's toga. "Where is Chris? What's going on?"

With a sigh, Persephone grabbed Grace by the wrists and pulled her fingers off the delicate fabric. "Chris is being taken back to the Underworld," she informed.

Grace's eyes blurred with unshed tears. "No, please. You can't let Hades do this!"

The Goddess folded her arms across her chest. "I can, and I will. The bargain Hades agreed to was more than most people ever get as it is. Now that deal is broken. Chris is moving on. He will feel no pain, no sorrow. He is free now. Would you take that from him again? Are you that selfish?"

Grace closed her eyes and told herself to be patient and think before she acted. As James often reminded her, rushing in just got people killed. Just as it did Chris. She struggled to her feet, trying to stay calm and focused.

One problem at a time.

"It just hurts," Grace whispered between breaths.

That was an understatement. It was as if her insides were on fire. Every fiber of her being screamed out in agony.

"Yes. It hurts you." Persephone's voice had an urgent edge that made Grace wonder what else had been going on. "Grief, pain, sorrow. Those things belong to the living. I suggest you get back to your body, before you lose many more people you love."

Grace swallowed. It was like broken glass sliding down her throat. Persephone continued to hold her by the arms, as if to prevent some kind of tantrum.

"Persephone, promise me you'll look after Chris. I told him I'd restore his memories. Can you do that for me? Would you speak to Mnemosyne?"

Persephone let go of Grace's arms and then laid a gentle hand on Grace's cheek. "I swear it will be done. Now go save our brethren."

With a quick movement, Persephone drew back a hand and brought it forward like a snake strike, slapping Grace in the face.

* * *

GRACE lurched forward in her bed.

Coughing, she struggled to draw air into her burning lungs. Soon she realized that someone was pounding on her back.

"James?" she asked.

He smiled, relief spreading across his face. "The one and only."

Grace looked around her bedchamber. "Where's Chris?"

Hermes and Eros shot each other a nervous glance.

"He's gone." James backed up and slid off her bed. "Hades took him."

"What was he doing here?" Grace demanded. "Why wasn't he in Faerie?"

James gave a rather sheepish look. "I didn't know what else to do. You were dying. I thought if you heard his voice, it would bring you back. I wasn't sure you could hear anyone else, but I knew you would be able to hear him."

Grace was too numb to be angry. The pool of rage inside her lay quiescent, like a tranquil lake.

"You sacrificed him, to save me," she said without inflection. It was not an accusation, just a fact.

James folded his arms across his chest. "I would have done whatever it took to bring you back. Surely you, of all people, can appreciate that."

She did. After all, she had once risked the lives of every God and Fae to rescue James from Lilith.

Grace took a deep breath.

She had lost Chris. Again. She counted to ten in an effort to get the idea of pummeling Hades to death out of her head. Then she counted to ten again, staring at the ceiling to keep tears from spilling down her face. There would be a time to figure out some way to fix this, but not now. Killing Hades was not an option, as much fun as it sounded. Someone needed to put an end to the current violence or there would be nothing for Chris to come back to. Nothing for any of them to go back to.

Sliding her legs off the bed, she looked around the room. She took a shaky step, but pitched forward into the waiting arms of James. She looked into his eyes and saw worry there. Not a big surprise. She didn't exactly have the most rational track record when it came to Chris.

"I'm sorry," James whispered.

He could have said a million things to her. There were more than enough justifications and rationalizations. Maybe once he would have fed them to her as an object lesson. But this time he didn't. Those two simple words told Grace more than a thousand lessons could.

She leaned her forehead against his chest and wrapped her arms around him. "I understand," she said with all the love she could muster. "I forgive you."

Love was not always romance and flowers. Sometimes it was

a friend's embrace in a time of need. Someone to trust. Someone whose happiness took priority.

She felt the gentle tendrils of James power humming along her skin. Warm and tingly, it reminded Grace of home. She stepped back, releasing him and breaking the link with the power he was sending to heal her.

Behind Grace, a bright white light flashed.

In the blink of an eye, James was thrown against the far wall.

Grace spun around to see Prometheus standing there, his eyes burning gold.

"Get away from my daughter!" he bellowed, the room shaking with the timbre of his voice.

"Hold on," Grace pleaded. "It's okay."

Prometheus pushed her aside and raised one hand high, manifesting a huge energy ball to strike James who struggling on the floor.

"No!" Prometheus bellowed. "The Guardians have chosen sides! They stand against us! He's here to take you back to them!"

"Brother, please," Hermes pleaded, but the look on his face showed blatant disobedience. He still wore military garb, and each hand held a glowing ball of power.

Prometheus silenced him with a look.

With a growl, Hermes fell to his knees, the energy balls vanishing as he struggled against invisible bonds.

James got to his feet. Where his gray shirt was burned the skin showed through in red welts. "Grace, Prometheus is the one who drained your powers. He's been using the Eye of Hera to siphon your powers for himself." James pointed at the Prometheus. "He's the reason you almost died."

Grace looked at her father, expecting nothing less than denial. She was not disappointed. She also was not buying the act. Not anymore.

"He's lying, Grace," Prometheus said, keeping his eyes fixed on James who was still shaky on his feet. "The Guardians are trying to turn you to their side. You can't trust them. You have to trust your family."

"Grace, please," James begged. "You know I would never lie

to you."

Grace hadn't yet decided how to deal with her father and she didn't want to tip her hand. She just blinked, trying to tell James without words that she trusted him.

Eros stepped between James and Prometheus.

"Move," Prometheus commanded.

"No. James is right." Eros' eyes narrowed at the Titan. "Someone has been draining Grace. I didn't realize it until today. She almost died, Prometheus. And here you stand with your full powers, when you should be as weakened as the rest of us. So tell me, how did you get your powers back if not by draining your daughter?"

"How dare you accuse me?" Prometheus raged, throwing the energy ball in his hand.

Eros was thrown into the wall so hard that chunks of stone exploded. A crack climbed up the wall like a lightning bolt, splitting the ceiling. For a second, the air was thick with dust and black feathers. When it cleared, Eros lay on the floor, his eyes closed. One wing was snapped nearly in half, the feathers either missing or singed off, and there was a gaping bloody notch the size of a cannonball cut of his side. Like macabre snowflakes, jet-black feathers drifted to the floor.

Stunned, Grace saw but didn't hear the command James gave Hermes.

James launched an energy ball at Prometheus, distracting him just long enough for Hermes to slip behind her and wrap Grace in his arms.

Before she could struggle to escape or rush forward to stop the fighting, they were gone.

CHAPTER 19

It was built against the immortal will of the gods,
and so it did not last for long. ~ Homer

LYNX took Phoenix's hand and pulled her up from the icy surf. The waves beat at their backs, as they waded to the sandy beach.

Phoenix shivered. The heavy wet gown made her steps uneven.

Lynx knew Phoenix well enough to read her troubled expression like a book.

Did Phoenix feel as if she had let Grace down? That she had broken the promise to protect her niece? At this very moment, Grace was at the mercy of the Olympians. Of course, no one could have ever dreamed that the old grudges would ignite into full-blown war.

As they walked, Lynx took her hand and pulled it to his chest.

Phoenix didn't protest. What was the point of standing on protocol now? They had abandoned Faerie.

He should have been back at the palace with the other guards, but Phoenix had been determined to leave. He had always regretted his decision to stay behind the last time she went to the human world. He would not make the same mistake twice.

With a Halberd drawn in his free hand, Lynx scanned the area. The biggest risk had been that Olympians would be guarding the Gateway. So far, there was no sign of them. Sensing no immediate danger, he used his powers to shrink the huge blade to only a few inches and then tacked it on his belt.

He looked around at small groups of tourists. With the exception of one old man who stared at them as if they were aliens, no one seemed to have witnessed their watery assent from the North Carolina Gateway. But Phoenix's soaked gown and his leather vest and pants were getting some strange looks now.

No time to worry about that, he thought. His first responsibility was to get Phoenix to safety.

It was not just the Olympians who would be after them now, but the Fae as well. It was chaos in Aletheia, everyone arguing and nothing getting done. The Gods had them trapped.

They took a huge risk leaving Aletheia, but Phoenix had made up her mind. End of conversation. She was going after Grace. Period. Never mind that the Fae would brand them both as traitors and that they might never be able go home. Phoenix was going and Lynx would follow her to the ends of the Earth, into the gates of Hell itself, before he would lose her again.

The Horse Island Gateway was only recently rediscovered by the Fae, and it was several feet underwater thanks to land erosion.

They climbed over the dunes and beyond the wary eyes of the humans before they stopped.

Phoenix lifted her head skyward, the soggy tendrils of her black and red hair clinging to her face and shoulders. "Hermes!" she called.

They waited.

Phoenix's nose crinkled in annoyance. "Where could he be?"

"Perhaps, he is ignoring your call." Lynx paused for a moment. "Perhaps he has become our enemy."

Phoenix snorted. "No. He must be doing something very important to ignore a call from me. He'll catch up to us when he can."

"You sound very confident," Lynx said, raising an eyebrow. He detested that Phoenix held the Messenger God in such high esteem. To Lynx, the Olympians were an annoyance at best and a dangerous enemy at worst.

"Look," she said, poking a finger into his sternum, "I trust Hermes. He's never let me down."

The words were like a knife in Lynx's gut. She was inferring that in the past a God was there for her when he wasn't. And she was right.

Lynx inclined his head. "Fine. For now let's get away from here and find some less conspicuous clothing."

They were indeed going to draw a crowd as dressed, and that

was not a good idea.

"Okay. I'm sure there are some shops along the boardwalk. Let's go." Phoenix took the lead.

After walking in silence across the island, they boarded the small boat that would ferry them to the mainland.

As Phoenix predicted, there were quite a few small shops catering to the crowds of summer tourists. Now late fall, the crowds were thinned to the point of non-existence.

They headed into a store that carried a wide variety of clothes and made their way through the racks.

Phoenix grabbed a red sundress and matching jacket.

Unfortunately, clothing selections in Lynx's size were harder to come by. They ended up with a pair of navy blue board shorts and a T-shirt that read 'Life's a Beach'. When she showed him the selections, he rolled his eyes but took the clothes from her outstretched hand, heading for the changing room that consisted of a tent-like structure made of curtains. It didn't inspire feelings of privacy. He slipped into the ridiculous clothing and slid the shrunken Halberd into his pocket. It would be hard to reach quickly, but there were not many options.

Lynx stepped out of the changing tent and turned slowly to get her approval on the clothing. "Shall I glamour the clerk for these?"

"No need. I've got something better than magic." Phoenix smiled and pulled a credit card from the pocket of her gown. She handed it to him and then ducked into the tent with her own change of attire.

CHAPTER 20

*Lost, I was leaving behind familiar paths, at
a run down blind dead ends.* ~ Virgil

"WHERE are we?" Grace asked, blinking against the bright sunlight.

Hermes offered a feeble grin. "Bern, Switzerland. I felt it was appropriate somehow."

They were in an empty playground. Despite a crisp chill in the air that warned of oncoming winter, Hermes wore his usual Hawaiian shirt, cargo shorts, and flip-flops. Olympians were the kings of the instant clothing change.

"We have to go back!" Grace demanded, unable to erase the sight of black feathers falling from the sky. "Eros was hurt."

"No," Hermes said holding her by the arms. "Eros will survive. James said to get you somewhere safe. I'm sure he and Eros have already gone elsewhere. You can't let Prometheus get his hands on you again."

Grace flopped into a swing seat and kicked the rocky ground with the tip of her boot. Hermes was right. She didn't like it, but she trusted James to get Eros somewhere safe.

Of course, she had trusted Prometheus, too.

"Why did he do this to me?" Grace knew the answer even as she asked the question.

It all made sense. She knew why she had been so tired even though she should no longer need sleep. Prometheus told her it was just her body adapting, but that was just another lie.

Her hand went to her throat, her fingers searching for the necklace her father gave her. It was gone.

"I removed the necklace," Hermes informed. "I believe it contained some kind of energy that made you more susceptible to his influence. It seemed to be dulling you to everything else while amplifying his will over you."

"How could he do that?" she whispered.

Hermes sat in the next swing seat. "He must be in possession of the Eye of Hera, as James claims. It is the only object I know of that would allow him such transference of power."

"He must have taken it before we caught Samael." Grace's mind reeled. Prometheus had lied to her from the beginning. "What do we do now?"

Hermes took a deep breath. "Well, we need to alert the other Gods to what he's done. Try to turn them against him. It might be the only way to prevent war. But it won't be easy. Prometheus is very powerful." Hermes' face twisted with a look of disgust. "If he tells the others they can use the Eye of Hera to siphon your powers and replenish their own, they might like that idea."

"Of using me as a human battery." Grace tried to see each of their faces. Which ones could she count on for support? Which ones would sell her out and use her up? In the end, the numbers she came up with were less than encouraging.

"I will try to persuade them to our side," Hermes said. "But you must hide and stay hidden. Can you think of a safe place? Somewhere they wouldn't think to look for you?"

Grace thought for a minute. "I have a place in mind."

He looked at her from over the top of his sunglasses. "I'm not going to like this, am I?"

"I need to go see Hades," she said in a voice much bolder than she actually felt. "I can hide out in the Underworld."

Hermes shook his head so hard his glasses almost fell off. "If you think I'm going to take you down there so you can go off half-cocked on some rescue mission to get Chris back, then forget it."

"No," Grace said. "Chris is gone. I won't try to get him back. But there's someone I need to talk to. I have to know the truth, and there's only one person who might give it to me."

Hermes tilted his head, as if considering the idea. "I suppose it's as good a hiding place as any. But stay away from Hades until I can figure out which side he's on, okay? And absolutely no going to see Chris. Understand?"

She crossed her heart.

"All right," Hermes replied. "I can take you as far as the shore. You get in and stay put, until I come for you. Do not, I repeat, do not do anything stupid. And you'll need this." He held a golden leaf in his outstretched hand.

"Define stupid," she said, taking the leaf.

Hermes glared at her for a moment. Then with a quick nod, he took her hand.

* * *

IN a flash Hermes was gone.

Grace stood alone on the bank of the river Acheron. She didn't have to wait long.

Just as the last glow of sunlight fell over the horizon, Charron appeared, rowing his small decrepit boat through the mist.

His jolly appearance and kind demeanor didn't match the way the Ferryman of the Dead was usually depicted. He was less skulls and crossbones and more Santa Clause. Except for the smell. Santa should smell like milk and cookies, but Charron reeked of mildew and dampness with a hint of something sour.

"Grace, it is so nice to see you again."

"You too, Charron. I need a ride."

"Do you have payment?" he asked with a menacing flash in his eyes.

She held out the golden leaf.

He took it, sniffed it, and then tucked it into his robes. With a laugh, he tapped his pocket. "For later."

The last time she handed him a golden leaf, he stuffed it in his mouth like it was the last candy bar on Earth. Now he was saving it for a snack.

Grace stepped gingerly aboard the boat, feeling good about her decision. The rotted wood creaked under her feet, as Charron pushed off the shore with the end of his long pole.

"So what brings you to the bowels of hell today?" he asked as cheerfully as a door greeter at some local discount store.

"I'm going to Tartarus," Grace answered.

"Aren't we all?" he replied with a hearty laugh.

The rotted meat smell hit her hard, as they glided through the murky water into the mouth of the cavern. Grace grabbed the railing for support and tried breathing through her mouth, but it only made her stomach churn harder. The smell slid down her throat like molasses.

Finally, a gentle sway told her they had reached the shore.

The last time she had entered the Underworld, James had been there. It was good to know she was strong enough to go it alone, although she would have welcomed the support.

"Thanks," she said.

She stepped off the boat and onto the rocky ledge.

Charron chuckled. "You must be the only person who has ever thanked me for bringing them to the Underworld."

Grace shrugged. "Yeah, I guess I'm weird like that."

Appraising the path in front of her, Grace squinted to see in the dim gray light. Squaring her shoulders, she walked into the land of the dead, hoping she would be able to find her way back home.

CHAPTER 21

Hateful to me as the gates of Hades is the man who hides
one thing in his heart and speaks another. ~ Homer

IT was easy to get lost in the maze of tunnels that made up the Underworld.

Grace walked for what felt like hours. Her legs burned, her eyes ached, and her mouth felt like the Mojave Desert.

On the verge of collapse, she stopped and leaned against a clammy grotto wall. She must have wandered for hours and had accomplished nothing except getting herself thoroughly lost.

"What are you doing here?" a velvety female voice asked. "You're supposed to be saving my husband."

Grace recognized the voice. Turning, she saw Persephone.

"I am," Grace replied. "Or I'm trying to. Hermes is rallying the Gods to stand against my—against Prometheus." She would never call him Father again. "I'm here because there's someone I need to talk to. Just for a few minutes."

Persephone tilted her head to the side. "This had better not be some stupid ploy to see Chris again."

"It's not," Grace swore. "I need to see Samael."

Persephone straightened. The set of her jaw was tight. "He is in Tartarus."

"I know. I wouldn't be here if it weren't important. He may be the only person who can confirm whether or not Prometheus has the Eye of Hera. If so, Samael might be able to tell me what Prometheus plans on doing with it."

Persephone stood statue still. The floor beneath her turned from a patch of barren stone to a bright green carpet of moss with tiny white and purple flowers, that reached up from the ground as if she were the sun itself and they were trying to absorb her light. It was an amazing thing to witness.

After a few seconds of consideration, Persephone waved her hand. "Fine. Follow me."

Without another sound, Persephone turned and walked back down the tunnel, leaving a bed of soft grass in her wake.

Grace sucked in a deep breath and followed. She felt life radiating from Persephone. It was as if the power inside her extended out several feet from her body, engulfing everything around her in the primal energy of life. It grazed Grace as they walked and she found herself soaking it in like rays of sunlight.

Slowly, Grace's powers returned. She felt rejuvenated.

Now she understood what attracted Hades to Persephone. His wife offered an intoxicating contrast to the constant agony and death that surrounded him.

They wove in and out, tunnel after tunnel.

Just when Grace was about to give the typical 'are we there yet' speech, Persephone came to a swift halt and turned.

"This is as far as I will take you," Persephone informed.

Grace understood. Not as far as she *could* take her, but as far as she *would* take her. Whatever lay at the end of the hallway was bad. Extremely bad.

"Thank you Persephone, for everything," Grace said and meant it.

She hadn't forgotten that the Goddess had intervened on her behalf, giving her the amazing gift of a few more months with Chris. The fact that Grace wasted them was no one's fault but her own.

Persephone nodded, a grin playing at the corners of her mouth. Then she vanished. The only evidence she had been there was a small patch of grass, that began to shrivel and brown the moment Persephone disappeared.

Alone now, Grace could make out distant cries. Moans. The sound of someone in terrible pain. It was a sound she knew well. She had made a similar sound once. Preparing herself for the worst, she walked forward toward the screams. Toward the one person she had hoped never to see again.

As the sounds grew closer, Grace was surprised to notice a crackling in them, as if they were being played on an old-fashioned tape player. Stepping through the final doorway, she understood why.

It was a zoo. Not a 'come look at the cute panda' zoo, but a gruesome prison zoo. The grotto was massive. Loud speakers ran along the ceiling, projecting noises in stereo. Moving forward cautiously, Grace looked into the first window cut into the stone.

Inside a woman sat at a spindle. As fast as she spun thread, it unwound from the spindle and flowed back into a basket of wool. The woman was gaunt, her fingertips bloody. She slumped forward, her red eyes not blinking as she worked.

Grace took a step back and then eased to the next window. Two men stood back to back, both digging holes. As one tossed a shovel full of dirt out of his hole, it landed in the other ones. Over and over, each filled the one's hole, while trying to empty his own.

She continued moving down the line, searching for Samael. She tried not to look too closely. Some of the things happening in the cages were too awful to ponder. Others were gut-wrenching exercises in futility. There was one where she paused, horrified.

A man sat on the floor, weighted to the ground by a large chain around his ankle, as the tank slowly filled with water. Grace watched him panic, kicking and flailing as the water rose over his head. Startled, Grace stepped forward, pounding on the window's glass. The rational part of her brain knew this person was already dead, but something in her screamed to act. She could not just stand there while he drowned. She hit the glass as hard as she could with her closed fists, as the man convulsed and eventually grew still. In a gush, the tank emptied and the man lay curled on his side, water spewing from his nose and mouth as he coughed. She took a step back. Within moments the water was rising again.

What had all these people done to end up in such a terrible place?

With a heavy heart, Grace moved on, trying to keep her head down except for a quick glance at the person in each cage.

Grace knew her search was over when she spotted familiar Roman robes, the ones Samael wore when he dreamed of his human life as Julius Caesar. Now she watched as a group of friendly looking men surrounded him. They spoke for a minute and he laughed. Then without warning, a hand holding a dagger struck out like a snake and stabbed him in the back. On that cue, the whole group pulled knives and short swords from their robes and started stabbing him repeatedly.

Her stomach clenched, as she watched. By the time they were done, their hands and clothes were covered in dripping red blood and Samael lay face down in the mud, his eyes glassy. The men walked away. After a minute, Samael blinked and sucked in a huge breath. His clothes were once again spotless and the wounds gone, as he pushed himself to his feet.

Grace could not contain her shock. He was reliving the day he was murdered over and over. The day he was betrayed by his friends and family. The worst day of his life.

Considering the things he had done to James and some of the others, Grace understood the source of the punishment. At one time, if she would have known this was his punishment, she might have called it poetic justice. But seeing it happen over and over was different. Her heart ached for him. No matter his crimes, would no one step in and stop the punishment?

When was enough, enough?

Pushing aside sympathy, she banged on the window glass in order to get his attention. Then she realized it was a two-way mirror. She could see him, but he could not see her. Nor hear her, apparently.

She needed to get into the cage somehow. Again she pounded on the glass but with no success. She looked around for something to break the glass with, but found nothing. Then she got an idea.

Some glass, like tempered car windows, could only be shattered by a sharp point of impact. Grace patted her sides, but found nothing in her pockets. Absently, her hand went to a stone around her neck. It was small, in the shape of a crystal and it had a point at the end. It was a gift from Hermes, a protective bloodstone. She could not remember when she quit wearing it or why, or for that matter how she came to have it on now, but she was grateful she did.

That sneaky God must have slipped it back on me when he changed his clothes.

Grace smiled at the feel of the stone between her fingers and at the absolute faith and trust she had in her godly cousin. It was all about love and trust.

Snapping the chain with one smooth yank, she clutched the stone in her fist. With her back to the glass and her eyes closed, she swung her arm like a hammer and hit the glass with the point of the stone.

Crack!

Grace opened her eyes.

A huge spider web of cracks appeared in the window. Closing her eyes again, she swung once more. This time the glass shattered, pieces tinkling to the ground like raindrops.

Then a horrible sound erupted from the overhead speakers.

Stuffing the stone back into her pocket and shaking bits of glass from her hair, Grace turned and made eye contact with one very surprised Samael.

"I need to talk to you," she announced casually.

"You have my undivided attention," he promised, eying her with suspicion as he stepped through the broken window. "And my thanks."

Grace folded her arms across her chest. "I didn't do it for you. I need you to tell me about Prometheus."

"I did try to warn you, after all." Samael gave a smile rife with arrogance, as he dusted off his robes. Although he must have been quite handsome once, over the centuries he had taken on a vaguely serpent-like appearance.

"You know, I can call Hades down here and have him stuff you back in that cell."

"I'm sure someone will be here for me soon enough," he said, visiting with her like a friend chatting over tea. "What do you want to know?"

"Does he have the Eye of Hera?" Grace asked, using her shoe to clear a path in the broken glass so she could step closer.

"Yes," he confirmed. "He took it from me. We made a deal. He was supposed to convince you to help me. It looks like he betrayed us both." He walked to the next window and peered in at one of the other prisoners. "Oh my."

Understatement of the century.

"The Eye, can it be destroyed?" Grace asked, trying to keep him on the subject.

"Of course," Samael, not taking his eyes off whatever was happening in the next cell. "Though why you would want to do such a thing is beyond me. If you could get it from him, you could rule the Olympians. It's your destiny. You're the Harbinger, the one who will change everything."

"I'm not interested in destiny. I want that orb gone before it hurts anyone else. How do you destroy it?"

Now she had his attention. He took a step toward her. Grace noticed his feet were bare and that he was leaving bloody footprints on the floor. He must have walked right through the broken bits of glass.

"Oh," he said, noticing what caught Grace's stare. "No worries, dear. When I was brought here all my powers were stripped from my bones. Quite literally, mind you. These little scratches are nothing in comparison. As for destroying the Eye, I don't know exactly." He blew out an exasperated breath. "All I know is that it must be destroyed with forgiveness, whatever that means."

Grace stared at him for a moment, trying not to lose her temper. "Could you be a little more vague? Honestly. Real helpful there, Sammy. Can you at least tell me what he's up to?"

"Isn't it obvious? Prometheus wants to take over. If he gets his full powers back and gets the Olympians behind him, he could rule the world. No one could stop him."

"I can stop him," Grace said, sounding more confident than she actually felt.

Samael rolled his eyes.

In the distance, a low growl rumbled down the tunnel.

"Hellhounds," Grace muttered. "Just what I needed today."

"Get out of here," Samael said. "I'll distract them. Go on. Call for Hades to put me back and get going. You should be able to blink out of here."

The growling got louder.

Grace stared at him, stunned. "Why would you do that? And how do I know that you won't vanish the second I'm gone?"

"Because I can't," Samael said with a sigh. "My powers are gone, remember? And because I deserve to be here. I did terrible things, Grace. I forgot what it was like to care about anyone or anything besides myself. Godhood will do that to you. I'm sorry. Be careful. Now go!"

Distant growls morphed into a chorus of angry barking Hellhounds, and the sound was getting closer.

Grace looked in Samael's eyes and noticed a faint flicker of real regret. Arrogance had been stripped away, leaving behind this pathetic man. A man that made all the wrong choices, lost everything, and ended up here, alone and tortured for eternity.

As she stared into his eyes, she saw a little bit of herself. She touched him on the arm, a gentle and brief physical contact, but it was enough.

"Thank you," she whispered.

Samael patted her hand and then turned to face the oncoming beasts.

Grace knew she was supposed to wait for Hermes, but needed to get out of there. First, she must make sure someone kept the hounds from devouring Samael.

"Hades!" she yelled.

A picture of her home in Colorado formed in her mind.

One second the shadow dogs were rushing at her just as Hades appeared in full battle armor at Samael's side. The next she saw the familiar surroundings of her kitchen.

She slumped to the floor, emotionally and physically spent.

Resting her head on the cool linoleum, she cried.

She cried for her own stupidity. For her poor choices. For all the people she had loved and lost. For everyone she had hurt.

And she prayed she would not end up like Samael.

CHAPTER 22

*I was shattered, I dragged out my life in the shadows,
grieving, seething alone, in silence.* ~ Virgil

"ENOUGH," James huffed, pulling Grace to her feet. "Get up."

Wiping her eyes with the back of her sleeve, she sniffled. She threw her arms around James, squeezing him tightly. "Are you okay? I was worried. And Eros?"

He patted her back and then stepped out of her grip. "I'm fine. He's fine too. Just a little scratched up."

"Scratched up? There was a hole in his side this big." Grace made a circle the size of a melon with her hands.

"We heal quickly, remember?" James glanced at the front door. "Uh, listen, you should prepare for company."

Just then, Hermes appeared inside the front door with Phoenix is his arms. He eased Phoenix to her feet and gave a smile. "Be right back."

Phoenix and Grace rushed into each other's arms, colliding with a mutual *oof.*

A moment later, Hermes returned, holding the shoulder of a downright surly-looking Lynx, who sported cobalt blue board shorts and a bright T-shirt stretched too tightly over his bulky arms and chest.

"What?" Hermes asked with a smirk. "I'm just saying I think this is a good look for you. That's all."

With a scowl, Lynx brushed Hermes' hand from his shoulder.

When Phoenix began to wheeze for lack of air, Grace opened her arms and took a step back. "How did you get out of Faerie?"

"We took the Horse Island gateway," Phoenix explained. "Luckily, there were no guards posted. I doubt the Olympians knew about it at all."

Lynx pointed at Grace. "Your father just started a war."

Phoenix smacked away Lynx's hand and shot him a stern look. "It's not Grace's fault. We all trusted Prometheus." She reached out and smoothed down Grace's hair. It was a something she had done since Grace had been a small child. "I'm so sorry, sweetheart. Hermes told us what happened. If I'd had any idea what Prometheus was up to, I wouldn't have let him within a hundred feet of you."

Grace took Phoenix's hands. "It's not your fault. Like you said, we all trusted him. It's my fault, partially at least. If I hadn't made that deal with Hades, the Fae never would have flown off the handle and the Olympians wouldn't have an excuse to pick a fight. All we can do now is deal with it as best we can."

"Where is Chris?" Phoenix asked, looking around. "I went to tell him we were leaving, but he was gone. I figured he would be with you."

Grace winced.

"Uh," Hermes moaned. "I may have neglected to mention that part."

"He's gone," Grace said, tossing her hands in the air. "In the Underworld. For good this time."

James stepped forward. "When Grace was unconscious, I feared she would die. I convinced Chris to come to Olympus and help us bring her back. It worked, but it was only a matter of minutes before Hades tracked him down."

Phoenix glanced from Grace to James and then back again. "Oh, I'm so sorry, Gracie."

Grace took a deep breath. "So am I. But here we are. And right now we need to focus on bringing this war to an end."

Hermes grabbed a wooden chair and sat at the kitchen table. Everyone else followed suit.

"I've gathered half a dozen Gods to our side," Hermes informed. "So, what's the plan?"

Everyone looked at Grace, even James.

Be worthy of the trust they are putting in you, she told herself.

"Before we go against Prometheus," Grace warned, "we need to separate him from the Eye of Hera. As long as he has it, we're too vulnerable."

"Agreed," Hermes said. "But how do we get close enough to steal it without him using it on us?"

"We get him to bring it out into the open," Grace replied. "Then we have to get him to use it. On me."

"Time out," James said, making a T-sign with his hands. "Bad plan. We need you at full power, not giving another dose of Super Grace Juice to our enemy."

"He's right," Phoenix agreed.

Grace took a minute to think about what James was saying. "No, Prometheus trusts me," she said after a moment. "Or at least, he thinks he has me so under his spell that I'll believe anything he says. I think I can get close enough without him suspecting anything. Then when he moves to drain me, you guys make with the *kaboom* and sticky finger the orb."

Lynx leaned across the wooden table. "How exactly are we supposed to get our hands on the orb? We can't just take it out of his pocket."

Hermes chair slid back and then he stood. "Leave that to me. Once I know where he's hiding it, I can teleport it out of there. But he can't be touching it or it'll pull him along with it. He has to let go of it. Just a second will do."

"I can get it away from him," Grace vowed.

James pulled a pinched face, as if he were trying to find a hole in her logic. In a moment, he relaxed and gave a deep shrug.

"Fine," Grace said. "Then here's the plan."

CHAPTER 23

To be trusted is a greater compliment than being loved.
~ George MacDonald

GRACE took a deep breath in through her nose and out through her mouth.

The scent of pine and salt hung heavy in the air. In the distance, Goat Island looked like something from a dream, as it skirted in and out of the mist covering the Puget Sound.

It held the most used gateway to Faerie, and Grace knew her father would be there. She wished Chris was standing behind her, lending his strength to hers. Though the others were just out of sight, waiting for her signal, Grace still felt alone.

Thoughts raced like lightning through her mind. How could her father do that to her? How was she going to put an end to this war? Why, once again, was it all falling on her shoulders?

More importantly, when all this was over how could she keep putting one foot in front of the other? How could she go on without the one thing that made her feel complete?

It was fear talking. She shook it off and focused on the task at hand.

Swallowing back the rising swell of emotions, she closed her eyes and took a step forward with a picture of Prometheus in her mind.

She opened her eyes, blinking hard against the green glow of the forest. The cistern, normally full to the rim with murky green water, was empty and surrounded by Gods. Eris, Hades, and Apollo held their hands over the edge of the well, stretching a blue cord between their fingers. It was a web of magic, holding the gateway closed.

Prometheus stood nearby, supervising the others. His white wings fluttered outside a black and gold vest, and he wore a pair of heavy boots with silver spikes on the tips. His pants were loose leather with strips of chain mail dangling from the waist.

Grace's desire to capture the Eye of Hera overwhelmed her revulsion of him. She rushed forward, throwing herself into her father's arms.

Prometheus stiffened. Then he wrapped Grace in a tight hug.

"Child, you are well once more," he said with a hint of surprise.

"Dad." She almost choked on the word. "I don't know what happened. I fell asleep. When I woke up Hermes was there telling terrible lies about you. I told him to let me go, but they took me to this place in Switzerland." Grace gushed out the story, her voice reaching a hysterical fever pitch. "It was awful. Dad, they killed Chris. They took him to Olympus knowing Hades would take him. They said the Fae weren't our enemies. But, dad, they put me in prison. My head is so foggy inside. I don't know what's going on with me. I came to find you as soon as I could. What's happening? I don't understand."

Prometheus just stroked her hair in a calming way.

It was all Grace could do to hold back the nausea that came with his touch. The tears falling from her eyes were real. They were tears of anger, hurt, and disappointment.

"There, there," Prometheus cooed. "It's all right now. You've been through so much my precious child. Come with me now. We will talk."

Grace nodded, sniffled, and leaned on Prometheus, as he walked them to a small moss-covered building down the path.

Once inside the building, Grace sat on a thick trunk of fallen log that was so spongy it squished beneath her. It was not hard to look wide-eyed and panicked, as she continued to sob.

Prometheus folded his thick white wings behind him and sat beside Grace.

"Are you all right?" he asked softly.

Grace wiped her hands down her face. "I feel like I'm going crazy. My brain is Swiss cheese. There are all these holes and gaps. I just can't seem to get a grasp on anything, you know? And what's going on with Hermes and James? They're acting like we're the bad guys. I just don't get it."

"I believe Hermes and James have chosen to defend the Fae. It is of little importance." There was an angry edge to his words. "Once they recognize that we are only doing what needs to be done, they will come back to us."

Grace nodded, leaning closer to him. "What can I do? I want to help."

Prometheus smiled. "You should just rest for now. Recover your strength."

"Oh, and that's the other thing. I tried to use my powers to get away from Hermes and James, but I couldn't. It was like there was nothing there. It took so long for everything to come back. I only just got away."

Prometheus' smile slipped a fraction, and then returned to a smooth line. "You're exhausted. Just try to get some rest. We're working to destroy the Gates, one by one. This is the last functioning gateway to Faerie. Once it is destroyed, they can never hurt us again."

"Please, Dad," she begged. "I just want to help."

"And help you shall, but not now. Now you rest."

Grace shrugged and leaned over, half-lying across the log. She closed her eyes. Waves of exhaustion tore through her. She fought them back, focusing on her breathing and keeping her senses stretched out around her. She felt the whisper of a breeze from the empty window hole behind her, feel the prickles of sunlight that dotted through the trees. A sticky sweet aroma filled her sinuses, as Prometheus bent over her. Then a soft glow filled her vision and she closed her eyes.

The Eye of Hera.

With one quick blast of energy, she blew an energy ball into the center of his chest.

Prometheus flew backwards into the far wall. The stone exploded as he hit. Falling through the rubble, he collided with the forest floor.

The Eye of Hera dropped from Prometheus' hand.

Faster than a blink, Hermes was there. In another blink, both he and the Eye were gone.

In a heartbeat, Prometheus was back on his feet, roaring. His eyes shone bright gold as he stalked forward.

Grace's mind went blank. Part of her screamed to defend herself, the other part warned her to run. But the rage boiling inside her screamed for her to stand her ground, screamed out for blood and retribution.

As her insides warred, Grace was left paralyzed.

A pair of strong hands grabbed her by the arms.

In a blink, the island was gone along with the image of her father.

* * *

GRACE stood once more in her own house.

"Are you all right?" James asked, giving her a shake. His face was etched with worry.

She blinked a few times, letting her emotions recede. "I'm fine."

"Good, and well done," Hermes said, holding the Eye of Hera in his outstretched hand. "This, I believe, is yours."

"Mine?" she asked.

Hermes nodded. "I don't think anyone else could be trusted with it."

With a shaky hand, Grace took the still glass orb. It looked so harmless, like a dim light bulb. As soon as she touched it, Grace knew otherwise. The instant it connected with her fingers a strange film seemed to cover her hand. It slid its way up her arm like ice water, chilling her flesh. Her first instinct was to drop it and wipe her hand on her pants.

Before the energy of the Eye could reach her elbow, Grace's powers surfaced from somewhere deep inside. Warm and tingling, it was nothing like the slimy cold power coming from the orb. Her power ran over her skin, chasing back the magic of the orb until it was completely contained in the glass ball.

"Whoa," Grace said.

"Exactly," Eros said, appearing from around the corner.

Grace rushed to him and hugged him tightly, careful of the bandage on his shoulder and the gauze wrapped around his injured wing.

"I was so worried about you," she said, giving him a quick peck on the cheek.

"I've been worse. He caught me off guard." Eros pointed at the orb. "If it wasn't for that, I would have shoved one of my lead arrows right up his—"

"Whoa!" Hermes held up his hands. "Too much visual there, buddy. I'm just glad you're all right."

Grace stepped away from Eros, leaving him to exchange a bone-crushing handshake with Hermes.

"All right," Grace said, getting back to the plan at hand. "Hermes and James go gather the Gods who are on our side. Now that we have the Eye, it will at least be a fair fight. Phoenix, you and Lynx must return to Faerie. Be careful. You'll have to go back through the Horse Island Gateway. The others, except for Goat Island, have been destroyed according to Prometheus. Tell them what's happening. Tell them we're trying to put an end to this. Get whoever you can out through the Horse Island Gateway. It's our safest bet at this point. If this comes down to a fight with Prometheus, I'll need all the help I can get."

"What are you going to do?" Phoenix asked.

"I need to figure out how to destroy this thing," Grace answered, lifting the orb to eye level.

Phoenix frowned. "I don't think we have time for that right now."

"I agree," Hermes chimed in. "We need you to set up a meeting with Prometheus and the others. Without the orb, they might be willing to make a deal."

Lynx took a step forward, his chiseled face stoic. "No deals. It has gone too far for that. War has been declared. If you want to make peace with the Fae, Prometheus must be defeated and a new treaty forged. The Council will never trust Prometheus. Someone else must lead the Olympians."

"He's right," Phoenix said, laying a gentle hand on Grace's shoulder. "The Olympians will need a new leader, a new representative. Someone the Fae can trust."

"Well, that rules me out," Grace said with a snicker.

"Not necessarily," James countered.

"That doesn't matter right now. What am I supposed to do with this?" Grace held the orb up again. "And don't say use it, because that isn't even an option."

"If we can't use it and we can't destroy it, then we need to hide it," James said. "Somewhere Prometheus won't be able to find it."

"How about somewhere Prometheus won't be able to 'retrieve' it?" a voice asked from the back of the room.

Grace turned and saw Hades striding into her kitchen. He still wore his jet-black battle armor beneath a long black cape. It would have been comical, if not so unnerving.

James stepped forward, positioning himself between Grace and the God of the Dead.

Grace was not sure if James was protecting her or Hades.

Lynx made a similar move, standing in front of Phoenix.

"It's all right," Hermes said, his hands raised in a gesture of peace. "He's with me. He's on our side."

"To clarify, I am on no one's side but my own," Hades said, setting his large metal helmet on the counter. "I answer only to the Mother Goddess, not some bloodthirsty Titan. I believe Prometheus must be stopped."

James opened his mouth to say something, but Grace stopped him with a stern glance.

"What are you talking about?" Grace asked, leaning around James.

"There is a place where the orb will be safe," Hades answered in his usual cryptic fashion. "And no one but Grace will be able to access it."

"If you're talking about the rift where Dora hid the Urn," Phoenix retorted in a sharp voice, "that isn't accessible for another thousand years."

"I'm not," Hades snarled in reply.

Grace stepped around James and looked Hades straight in the eyes. "Then what are you talking about?"

"You would trust me?" Hades asked, staring back as if he could see right through her.

She swallowed a lump of emotion the size of a golf ball and nodded. Hades was many things, but she didn't think 'liar' was one of them.

He stared at her for a moment. "There is a place sacred to the line of Oracles. Grace's line."

"I'm not an Oracle," Grace protested.

"Your mother was an Oracle," Hermes reminded in a gentle voice. "Your father was the God of Foresight. The Oracles are your lineage, like it or not. You may not be an Oracle yet, but it is in your blood."

Grace shivered. As Hades stood there, leaning against her counter, the room got colder. It was as if his mere presence drew life from the room. Behind him, a small potted cactus in the windowsill shriveled like a prune.

"The book of the Oracles is more than a record of their predictions," Hades informed. "It's a doorway into another place. In the past Oracles often kept objects, particularly objects of power, safe inside its pages. You could use the book to hide the orb. Then retrieve it when you figure out how to destroy it."

The room grew quiet, as all waited for Grace to make a decision. Did she trust Hades? Did she have a choice?

"All right, will you show me how?" Grace asked.

Hades gave a curt nod, which she returned in kind.

"Thank you," Grace said and turned to Hermes. "Where will we meet up?"

"James and I will gather our forces," Hermes informed. "We'll try to lure Prometheus away from the Gateway at Goat Island. We'll try to draw them to the Gateway in Virginia. James will work on repairing the gate, so the Fae can come through there and join us."

Grace nodded. "Okay everybody. Good luck."

James took Grace by the arm and pulled her aside. "Are you sure about this?" He hooked a thumb over his back toward Hades. "About him?"

Grace leaned in. "I trust Hermes. Hermes trusts Hades."

James let her go. "And I trust you."

Grace understood how hard those words were for James to

utter. He had been betrayed by everyone, it seemed. For him to trust Grace, considering her poor track record, required nothing less than a miracle.

Eros took Phoenix by the hand and vanished, followed by the others. The room was empty except for Hades and Grace.

"Do you know where the book of the Oracles is?" Hades asked in a sharp voice.

"Yep," Grace answered. "Prometheus gave it to me when I moved to Olympus. It's in my room there."

"Oh. Well, that will save us the time of having to search for it at least. Listen, this has to be in and out. You grab the book and go. Understand? I don't want to risk a confrontation with anyone yet, not until we are ready. And I will come, just in case we end up having to fight our way out."

Grace nodded.

Hades grabbed his helmet off the counter and stuffed it on his head as he vanished.

Grace took a deep, steady breath and followed.

* * *

GRACE and Hades arrived together at the entrance to Olympus.

They stepped into the archway and vanished again, re-appearing in Grace's temple room.

Hades stood by the doorway, keeping watch as Grace hurried into the small closet area where the large volume rested on a golden pillar.

The book lay open, its blank pages exposed.

Grace ran her fingers over the stark white paper. Then she flipped the book closed and tucked it under her arm.

Walking back into the main room, she gave Hades a curt nod.

With a sweep of his cape, he took her by the upper arm. "Let's go," he said in a husky voice.

Grace had only a moment to rethink trusting the lord of the Underworld before she was pulled away into the unknown.

CHAPTER 24

When life is more terrible than death, it is then the truest valor to dare to live. ~ Thomas Browne

GRACE stumbled, as she materialized inside Hades chamber in the Underworld.

It was pretty much the same as the last time she had been there, minus the ferocious hellhounds. It looked more like a playboy's bachelor pad than the executive chamber of the God of the Dead. A massive flat screen television was suspended in the center of the room with every game station imaginable stacked underneath in neat piles. The sofa and chairs were rich black leather. There was even a remote control on the side table. If he could hang a huge television in mid-air, did he really need a remote to control it?

"What are we doing here?" she asked, taking a step back from Hades.

"We needed somewhere safe for me to show you how to use the book," Hades explained in a cool, deep voice. "Prometheus wouldn't dare show his face here."

Grabbing the remote off the glass tabletop, Hades turned on the big screen and hit buttons until the television split into four sections. It looked like security camera footage.

The pictures changed too fast for Grace to follow.

After a few minutes, Hades stopped and enlarged one image to fill the screen.

"Ah, there she is." Hades turned to Grace. "Wait here. I'll just be a moment."

She watched as Hades stepped behind a large room divider to where she knew the three doorways to the Underworld stood. One door led to Tartarus, a second one to Elysium, and a third one to Asphodel. One realm was for the wicked. One was for the blessed dead. And the last door was for everyone else. She had once rescued Chris from the middle door, Elysium, which was where he was once again.

Being so close to that doorway was a test of her resolve.

Was Hades watching her from behind the divider? Waiting for her to take the opportunity to rush into another thoughtless bargain?

If so, he was about to be disappointed.

With a frustrated groan, Grace flopped down on the large leather sofa. The heavy book rested on her lap, as she turned the Eye of Hera in her hands. She leaned forward and studied the stone floor. It was smooth like glass, but stone nonetheless. With a shrug, she palmed the orb and slammed it into the floor as hard as she could. Once, twice, three times. She examined the orb. Not even a crack appeared.

She sat back with a sigh. Why couldn't anything ever be easy?

In a flash Hades was back, but he was not alone. There was a familiar woman beside him.

"Sybil?" Grace asked, surprised.

The former Oracle of the Dead had been imprisoned in a jar by Apollo. Grace convinced him to release her spirit. As payment for that favor, Sybil had guided Grace, James, and Lorna through the Underworld and straight to Chris.

Grace never expected to see the beautiful woman again.

Sybil was small and fragile looking, a mere wisp of a girl. She was slender with sharp features and long billowy blonde hair. She looked all of thirteen. The last time Grace saw Sybil she was ghost-like, insubstantial. But now she was flesh, standing barefoot in a bright blue sundress.

"Who better to teach you how to use the book than a former Oracle?" Hades said.

Grace had rescued Sybil from Apollo's curse so she would have a peaceful afterlife, not so she could continue to be used by the Gods.

"But she is supposed to be resting," Grace complained.

Sybil stepped forward and took Grace by the hand. "It's all right, Grace. I want to help you. An Oracle is a beacon of light in the darkness, a voice of reason in the chaos. The world should never be without one. If I had known you would be the next, I would have sought you out and trained you properly, as was my obligation. Hades has explained that time is precious. We must be swift. So I will give you an abridged instruction for now."

Grace wanted to protest. She was not an Oracle, no matter what anyone said. Her life was complicated enough without adding more fuel to the fire.

Before she could say anything else, she heard Phoenix's voice in the back of her mind: *Sometimes, you just do what you have to do to get the job done.* As always, Phoenix was right.

Grace swallowed hard. "Fine. Show me what to do."

The contrast of Sybil's pale white skin against thin red lips and wide dark eyes made her resemble a doll. Her hair, a mass of golden waves, was expertly woven up the back of her head with blue ribbon until it spilled out the top, framing her face.

Sybil motioned for Grace to set the book on the table in front of her. Grace slid the tome off her lap onto the glass surface, where it flipped open to the middle.

"Hades," Sybil said, turning toward him. "I'm sorry, but this will require privacy."

Instead of giving his usual snotty retort, Hades pushed off from the wall against which he was leaning. He bowed once to Sybil and then vanished.

"Wow," Grace whispered.

Sybil smiled. "Hades is one of the few Olympians who has respect for the powers of the Oracles. Shall we begin?"

Grace found it hard to imagine Hades having respect for anyone. But then her experience with him was limited. Limited to her wanting to slap him silly most of the time.

"Yes," Grace answered. "Please."

"Look at the page and tell me what you see," Sybil instructed.

Grace leaned over, examining the page carefully. She looked at it like one of those three-dimensional posters where an object pops out at you if you look hard enough. She stared until her eyes crossed. She could make out the small fibers in the paper, but there was no trace of ink or even hidden impressions. She finally blinked and sat back with a sigh.

"I see nothing," Grace admitted. "It's blank."

"Yes, it is," Sybil smiled.

Grace tilted her head. "What?"

"It is blank. There is nothing written on this paper."

"Then how am I supposed to read it?"

"You aren't."

"Okay, not to be rude, but I really don't have time for cryptic games."

"It's no game," Sybil said. "There is nothing on the paper. No words. There are images inside the paper."

Grace lifted a page, examining it between her fingers. It was thin, as it should be. She dropped the page. "I don't understand."

"Put your hand on the page," Sybil instructed.

Grace wiped her hand down her pants and then obeyed. "Okay. Now what?"

"Close your eyes. Good. Now focus on the tactile sensation of the paper under your hand."

Grace did as she was told.

"Yes, that's right," Sybil continued. "Clear your mind. See yourself standing in an empty room with white walls. A blank space."

Grace imagined herself standing in a room with white walls, no windows or doors. She tried to focus on her hand until it was the only sensation in the world. Everything else fell away.

She almost opened her mouth to ask what to do next when she felt the rush overtake her. She was an empty vessel in an empty room that began to be filled with images. It was similar to what happened when she had a vision. The static came first, like a television on the wrong channel. Slowly it faded into a series of images. A man being thrown from a horse. *Flash.* An old woman lying in bed, surrounded by small children singing to her in a language Grace didn't recognize. *Flash.* A man in Greek robes being dragged down a dirt street and thrown into a dirty cell. Flash. A young mother holding two infants in her arms.

Grace felt her hand pull back from the page and the images stopped. The room was empty again.

Grace's eyes flew open. "What was that?" she asked, breathless.

"The record of what that Oracle saw on that day."

"It was so much."

Sybil gave a wan smile. "It was not always that way. Some Oracles were sent among the humans. They were often bombarded with tasks, questions, requests. Some of them were fortunate enough to see only for the Gods themselves. Their services were used much less, and their visions and prophesies recorded more fully and carefully."

Grace licked her dry lips. "Okay, I need to learn how to hide something inside the book."

"That is a fairly simple matter. Place one hand on the object, one hand on the book, and focus again on the white room. Once there, visualize the object you are holding inside the room. Place it there. Then leave."

"Okay, here it goes." Grace paused. "That is, unless you know how to destroy the Eye of Hera?"

Sybil shook her head. "I'm sorry. I do not. But it is courageous of you to attempt such a thing. Many would seek to use it for their own gain."

Grace nodded and closed her eyes, one hand clutching the orb and the other pressed on the book.

* * *

PHOENIX and Lynx arrived back in Aletheia wet, exhausted, and under heavy guard.

As expected, they were branded as traitors. How else could they have escaped the Olympians?

Phoenix held her head high, as they were marched through town. There was no normal bustling of the day. The roads were virtually abandoned. The only activity seemed to be coming from the palace. Phoenix paused, missing a step. Lynx, who had been a step behind, was now at her side. She looked over her shoulder at him.

His strong face was grim. Ever the protector, he glanced this way and that, watching for any sign of attack.

They both knew coming back could mean a death sentence, but Grace needed them to do whatever they could to get the Fae on board with her plan.

Reaching over, Phoenix took Lynx's hand.

He looked at her, his face softening as their eyes met.

She had loved Lynx from the time they were very young. They sparred together as warrior children often did during training. It was an unwritten rule that Unseelie children always threw the battle with a Seelie child. It was a safety issue. As sad as it was, the life of a Seelie was simply considered more important than the life of a lesser Fae. Thus, the Unseelie would have to back down, take the loss, rather than risk hurting a Seelie.

On their first day of sparring, Lynx had without mercy knocked Phoenix on her back and disarmed her. When she asked him why, he explained that if he let her win then she would never learn how to defend herself. From that day on, she sparred only with Lynx.

As they grew, the sparring matches became as much verbal as physical. One day she ran into Lynx as he was cleaning out the palace horse stalls. There they shared their first kiss. For years afterward, they stole every possible moment together.

Then he was promoted into the service as a guard for the Queen, and their time together grew more infrequent. After Dora died, Phoenix was left to raise Grace. It broke her heart to leave Lynx behind, but she thought the separation would help her get over the feelings she carried for her childhood sweetheart.

And it had worked. Or so she thought.

Coming back to Aletheia, those old feelings rushed back to the surface. Now here they were, preparing to face down the entire Fae council, and all Phoenix could feel was gratitude that he stood beside her. For the first time, she didn't care about Seelie or Unseelie. She didn't care about their rules or their judgments. Some things were worth fighting for, dying for. Love was one of those things. Grace tried to tell her that once, but she didn't listen. Now all she could do was hope that she would have the time to make things right.

Lynx squeezed her hand and pulled it to his chest, holding

her hand over his heart.

She could feel Lynx's pulse racing under her fingertips. He didn't have to say a word. Neither of them did. Sometimes in silence everything was clear. No words were necessary.

They walked hand-in-hand up the stairs, as the guards led them into the massive amphitheater in the back of the palace.

People crowded the rows of bench seats, murmuring.

As Phoenix and Lynx were brought in, a hush crawled through the auditorium. In the center of the massive room, Philip stood at the podium and raised his hands in a request for silence.

"Well, I see our wayward queen has returned," a voice rang out. The acoustics of the room were such that anyone standing in its center could speak at a whisper, but their words would carry to every corner.

Phoenix ignored him and proceeded toward the center of the room. She needed to be heard by everyone.

Philip seemed to sense what she was doing.

"Guards, take her to her room," he ordered.

Before they could move, Lynx stepped forward dropping Phoenix's hand and called out. "Your Queen wishes to speak at assembly. Despite what has happened, it is still her right."

Phillip paled as a murmur of approval swept through the crowd. He took a step back and motioned for Phoenix to take the floor.

Within confidence, Phoenix moved into position. "I have been called a traitor. This accusation is untrue and unjust. I left Faerie not to aid those who have declared war on us, but to determine the severity of the situation. And to assess our best chances of winning this battle." She paused, scanning the mass of faces. "The Olympians have been divided. Prometheus has led an attack on us, on our very gates. But there are those who stand against him, those who even now seek our help in defeating him and his followers."

"How are we supposed to fight?" a voice called out from the audience. "We are trapped here."

"We are not trapped," Phoenix replied. "There is one gate that has been overlooked. As we speak, the Guardian James is working to repair another."

"He's a traitor too!" another voice yelled.

As if on cue, Michael stepped forward and stood beside Phoenix.

"No, the Guardians are impartial," Michael said in a smooth voice. "James has not chosen sides. He is working to re-establish peace. Just as I have been here speaking with you to work out a resolution, he has been negotiating with the Olympians."

With a sneer of contempt, Philip folded his arms across his chest. "Then why did he help the girl escape?"

"Because it was never appropriate for us to imprison Grace," Phoenix answered. "The Olympians only resorted to violence, because of her treatment. We would have done no less if it had been one of ours captured by them. Don't you see? Our actions gave them the excuse to challenge us. This war is as much our fault as theirs."

"Yes," Michael agreed. "If you had left the Guardians to judge Grace for her actions, as was our right and responsibility, this situation could have been avoided. It is time for us to own up to our mistakes and move forward. I suggest you reinstate Phoenix as regent and do as she suggests."

"Please, friends." Phoenix held out her arms. "The world as we know it is changing. It can be a world of lingering hate and war, or we can step up now and put an end to the conflict. We can shape the future here this day." Phoenix stepped back beside Lynx. "I can only hope our actions will be the right ones."

Philip moved back to the podium.

"Fellow Fae," Phillip began. "Our Queen has made a heavy request of us. She asks us to show forgiveness to those who have wronged us. She asks us to leave the safety of our homes and fight at the side of those who have been our enemies, to raise our weapons to secure a future of peace. I leave it to the judgment of the assembly. What say you?"

"Aye," a clear voice echoed.

"Aye," said another.

Soon the room was a chorus of "Ayes."

Philip snapped his fingers. From the corner, a woman walked

forward, carrying a pillow on which rested the royal crown. Philip took the crown and raised it to the assembly. Then he placed it on Phoenix's head.

"Majesty," Phillip whispered, leaning forward. "You must know I wish you no ill will. My concern has always been only for the safety and sovereignty of our people. I offer my sincere apologies if I have been vigorous in that defense."

Phoenix glared at him. His words seemed sincere enough, but she could not get past how easily he allowed the frenzy to overwhelm his better judgment. She turned to face the crowd.

They cheered.

"Thank you," Phoenix said. "Now, all who are able to fight gather at the east gateway. I will lead the way myself."

As the Fae departed, Michael approached Phoenix.

"Baal and I have been trapped here as well," Michael reminded. "Please, fill us in on the specifics of your plan."

Phoenix nodded. "Hermes and James are gathering the Olympians who don't support Prometheus. Grace has recovered the Eye of Hera and is hiding it from the others. It will be a battle, but hopefully a short one."

"Goddess help us," Michael muttered.

CHAPTER 25

Call no man happy 'til he is dead.
~ Aeschylus

CHRIS laughed, as he watched a young girl with bouncy gold curls chasing a bright blue butterfly through the meadow.

"Don't laugh at me," she fussed with a pout. "This is much harder than it looks, you know."

"Oh, I believe you," he said with a chuckle.

"Try it," she demanded in a twinkling voice.

"Watch and learn," he instructed.

Moving to the center of the field, he sat down in the tall grass so only his head was visible. He licked his palm and held it over his head.

The little girl watched in silence as the large purple and black butterfly flew straight toward him, landing in his hand.

"Come see," he said, motioning to the girl with one finger.

She bounced toward him happily, her white dress flapping in the gentle breeze.

"How did you do that?" she asked as he held the butterfly out to her.

"They like the salt in your saliva," he whispered. "It's licking it off my hand."

"It's so beautiful. Have you ever seen anything so beautiful?"

Chris opened his mouth to say no, then an image popped into his head. A girl with dark green eyes and a perfect heart-shaped mouth offered a coy smile half-hidden by long red hair spilling across her face. The image stole his breath. Then, as quickly as it had come, it vanished.

"Are you all right?" the girl asked, waving her hand in front of his face as he blinked.

"Oh, I'm fine," Chris replied, not entirely sure it was true.

The butterfly flew away.

"Oh, quick, catch it again!" she cried. "I want to take it home and keep it in a jar by my bed."

"Oh, you don't want to do that," he said gently. "If you keep it like that it will die."

"But I love it."

"Well, sometimes when you love something, you have to do what's best for it."

"Even if it makes me sad?" she asked.

"Oh, yes. Loving something means doing what's best for it, even if it makes you sad. Even if you want to keep it with you forever. The best way to love something is to let it go."

"I guess," she said, biting her lip.

"Okay," he said, rustling her golden curls. "Run along home before your momma misses you."

With a giggle, she slapped away his hand and ran off toward her family cottage.

Chris leaned back on his elbows and basked in the warm sunshine.

"She is a sweet little thing, isn't she?" a female voice asked from behind him.

Chris turned his head, squinting against the light. The woman's back was to the sun creating a glow all around her, making it hard to see her face.

"She's a little menace," he said playfully. "I don't think we've met before. I'm Chris."

He sat up, as woman sank to her knees beside him.

No longer illuminated by the sunshine Chris could see her more clearly. She had a long face with sun-bronzed skin and bright blue eyes. She wore a simple yellow dress that reminded him of the color of honey and was so close to the color of her hair that it was hard to tell where the hair ended and the gown began.

"Actually, I know who you are," she said. "I know everything about you."

Chris frowned, puzzled. "Have we met?"

"Not officially. You see, I'm in a bit of a bind. I'm looking for someone and I could really use your help."

"Well, who are you looking for?" he asked.

"You, of course."

Chris was truly puzzled now. "Then why do you need my help?"

"Oh, I'm so glad you asked," she said.

With a smile, she took his hand.

CHAPTER 26

The road to valor is built by adversity.
~ Unknown

"THE gateway should be functioning," James said, wiping his hands down his khaki pants.

"Good," Hermes said. "Now we just have to hope Phoenix can talk some sense into the Fae."

"If anyone can, it's Phoenix," James replied.

"True." Hermes had known Phoenix too long to believe she could ever fail at anything. The woman possessed nerves of steel and the courage of a lion. He had never admired anyone quite as much as he admired her.

"The others are on their way," Eros announced as he appeared on the edge of the vast clearing.

Hermes noticed that Eros was completely healed. Even his broken wing looked perfect again. That was good. They would need everyone.

"Husband, you forgot something," Psyche's fierce voice called from behind him.

"What?" Eros asked, reaching behind his back and touching the quiver of black arrows strapped between his wings.

"Me." Psyche wore full body armor made of thorny wood that moved as she did, as if it were cloth rather than bark. She smiled up at her husband. "If you think I'm going to sit at home while you fight, then you don't know me at all."

Eros wrapped his arms around his small, pale wife and kissed the top of her head. "I just want you to be safe." He sighed into her long curls.

"The safest place for me is by your side," she answered.

"We are here as well," Hades chimed in.

"I have your weapons," Hephaestus called out, carrying a

large gray sack as he approached the group. "They are my finest swords. They are not enchanted to kill, but they will be sufficient to disable the others. At least temporarily."

Hermes slapped him on the back. "Well done, brother."

Hephaestus smiled from the non-ruined side of his mouth.

"Well, someone planned a party and forgot to invite me," a sarcastic voice said.

Hermes looked up from the sword in his hand and into the face of Apollo.

Apollo looked every bit the sun god in his bright gold armor, his yellow blond curls crowning his face.

Behind Apollo, Eris appeared in head-to-toe silver-studded black leather strategically strapped to her neck, arms, and knees.

"Apollo, Eris, I have no wish to fight you," Hermes spoke as the others fell into defensive crouches. "None of us wants violence. You must see that Prometheus has led us astray."

"You gave your vow to obey and defend him as our leader," Eris hissed. "It is you who are the traitors."

"You are outnumbered two to one," Hermes said boldly. "The others have refused to get involved. It's six against three. The odds are not in your favor."

"True," Apollo agreed. "But unlike you, our powers have been restored."

"For how long?" Eros asked with a snort. "Prometheus lost the Eye of Hera. So how long until you burn through your stolen powers and are once more at our level?"

Eris pointed to the God of Lust. "It'll be long enough to teach you the price of treachery."

"Oh, we know all about treachery," Michael said, walking toward the group.

He was followed by no less than a dozen battle ready Fae, each wielding a halberd, some with two.

Behind Michael stood Phoenix, twirling one axe-like weapon in each hand.

Apollo took a step back. "Prometheus," he called into the air.

"How do you like the odds now?" James asked, manifesting an energy ball in each hand.

Prometheus appeared in the middle of the clearing, his eyes glowing gold. "You will not take my throne from me!" he screamed, drawing the sword hanging at his side.

Prometheus charged at Hermes, who just managed to deflect the blow.

Prometheus, Apollo, and Eris were nearly at their full powers, moving blurs to strike down body after body. The Fae circled and tried to surround them, but they were too fast.

Apollo laughed as he struck Lynx from behind, sending the large warrior sprawling face down in the grass. Before he could drive his sword into the fallen Fae, Phoenix stepped in and drove him back with a swing of her halberd.

"Apollo," she said, breathing hard. "I've been waiting for this for a very long time."

"As have I, Faerie," Apollo replied. "As have I."

"Psyche, go get Grace," Hermes demanded, as he exchanged blows with Eris. "We need her!"

Psyche nodded and vanished.

* * *

"THANK you Sybil," Grace whispered as the former Oracle stepped back through the veil into the Underworld and vanished.

In a flash of light, Psyche appeared. "The fight has begun," she said, taking Grace by the arm. "We need you. Now."

They vanished and then reappeared in the woods just a few yards from the fighting.

Without another word, Psyche ran through the brush and into the clearing where the fighting raged.

Closing her eyes, Grace visualized her bow and quiver. In a flash they were in her hands. She took a deep breath, strung her bow, and focused on the violence in front of her.

With a wordless scream Grace rushed forward, prepared to do whatever was needed to end the battle, even if that meant taking out Prometheus.

Her feet pounded the soft earth beneath her as she moved. Before she could make it beyond the last row of trees and into the meadow, the ground beneath her gave way. She felt herself falling. It happened so quickly there no time to scream, let alone reach out to stop her fall.

She landed with a solid thump, the wind knocked from her lungs. Grace pulled in a painful breath and then took in her surroundings. She was in a massive cavern. Large jagged crystals rose from the floor and hung down from the ceiling, as if desperately reaching for each other. The floor was damp. She looked up. The light from the hole though which she had fallen was a tiny dot far above her. If she had been human, the fall would have killed her.

Grace stood, scooping her bow from the cavern floor in the process. She dusted herself off and took a shaky, agonizing step.

Visualizing the meadow above, she tried to blink out. When she opened her eyes, she was still in the cavern. She tried again, this time thinking of her home in Colorado. Nothing.

What was going on? Was this one of her father's traps? How was she going to get out of this mess?

"James!" she yelled. "Hermes! Anybody!"

No response.

"Great," she mumbled to herself.

She looked around, trying to find something, anything that might be the key to her freedom.

"Oh dear, I do hope you're all right," a voice spoke behind her. "This part of Virginia is just full of nasty sinkholes."

She spun, bow drawn. "Who are you?"

The woman smiled, her honey gold hair flowing down her shoulders onto a matching dress. "Oh, no, no. None of that."

She flicked her hand and the bow vanished from Grace's hand.

Panicked, Grace opened her hands, trying to form the energy balls as she had been taught. Nothing happened.

"Yes," the woman purred. "You will find you are quite powerless down here. Not to worry. I'm not here to hurt you. I only want to talk." The woman gave a sweet smile and motioned for Grace to follow.

Unsure of what else to do, Grace cautiously obeyed. Whoever the mystery woman was, obviously she was way above Grace's level. Feeling very humbled by the display of power and more than a little eager to figure out a way out, Grace lowered her head and walked.

They followed a narrow passage into a vast cavern, much larger than the last one, where a massive crystal that looked like a praying angel rose up from the center of the chamber as if nature itself had carved it free from the stone.

They stopped, both admiring the formation.

From the ceiling droplets of water leaked from hanging crystals, landing in small pools on the ground. Grace felt the pressure around her change, as if the air was constricting around her. As Grace watched, the drops slowed to a trickle and then froze in mid-air.

Grace turned to the woman. She was obviously a Goddess. Was there a Greek Goddess of sinkholes? Whoever she was, she carried some serious power.

"Grace, I'm sorry for using such theatrics to get you here. You are a hard woman to get alone." The woman smiled, still staring at the crystal formation.

"Wait, the sinkhole was you? Of course it was. Look, there's a serious fight going on up there. I need to go help my friends."

"No. There isn't actually." The mysterious woman pointed upward. "As soon as you fell, time up there stopped. Or I should say slowed to a near stop. I wanted time to have a little talk. Just you and I."

Grace's mouth fell open. *Stopped. Time.*

"Who are you?" Grace asked.

The woman smiled and gave a casual shrug. "What's in a name? I've use so many. I am Goddess. The Mother. Gaia. Take your pick."

Grace felt the blood drain from her face. Standing with her in the near darkness was the Great Mother, the Creator Goddess. She and the Father created everything. Earth, Olympus, Faerie. She had put the divine smack down on the Olympians.

And now she was here.

Not good.

"What do you want with me?" Grace asked, not sure whether

she should bow or curtsey or drop to one knee.

"That's a complicated question," Gaia answered. "I want to know what you want."

Grace stilled. "I don't understand."

"Of course you don't. That's why I'm here." Gaia paused and gave a small frown. "I know you have a good heart. This is why you have such faith in the nature of the Olympians. It isn't their fault they've fallen so short. I am to blame for that."

Her instinct was to deny it, to comfort the Goddess. She was not sure why she felt that way, only that the desire was strong and deeply rooted.

"What do you mean?" was all Grace could manage to ask.

Gaia motioned for Grace to follow her as she walked around the stone angel. "You see, they were mortal once, every one of them. I mean the Olympians, of course. But my consort and I grew tired. We didn't want to leave humanity unprotected, so we selected the best of them and made them Gods, like ourselves. I didn't foresee the effect that kind of power would have on humans. Over time they became corrupted by it." She paused, reaching out to stroke what looked like a wing of the stone angel. "I finally had to step in, you see. But by then the damage was done. Once that type of power has been given, taking it away only fills them with rage. Some have adjusted well. Others, like your father, not as well."

Grace just nodded.

"And now here we are," Gaia said. "I have a problem, and you have the solution."

"I do?" Grace asked, stunned. Her base instinct was to throw herself at Gaia's feet and offer up whatever the Goddess wanted. It was a struggle to hold her composure and stay on her feet.

"I think so. And I am rarely mistaken about these sorts of things. So my question is what do you want."

Grace thought for a minute before answering. "Peace. I want to be able to end the fighting, to bring a truce back to my families. I want the people I love to be safe and happy."

"And what are you willing to do to achieve that?"

"That's a sneaky question," Grace blurted. "Hades asked me

that once, and he made me suffer for a long time."

Gaia frowned. She reached out and stroked Grace's hair. "I don't want you to suffer. You are one of my children, and I love you as much as your physical parents do."

As Gaia spoke, the words washed over Grace until she could feel love like a tangible thing, a blanket wrapped around her.

"But the universe requires balance in all things," Gaia added with a smile. "There can be no light without darkness, no joy without pain, no goodness without evil."

"I understand that," Grace said, a single tear slipping from her eye. In her heart she knew that she would do anything to end the fighting, anything to keep her loved ones safe, even from each other.

"I know you do. That is why I have an offer for you. If you accept it, I will give you a gift and a secret."

"What's the offer?" Grace asked, although deep down she knew didn't matter. There was nothing Gaia could ask that Grace would refuse.

"Don't look so scared, sweetheart." Gaia stroked Grace's hair again. "The offer is this. You can go back to your normal, human life. Mortal. Go to college, do whatever you were going to do before you were dragged into this world. Or you can remain here. Immortal. And take over the duties of the Oracle. You will be the partner of the Guardians. Help them help mankind. Think hard before you decide. Forever is a very long time."

The air rushed from Grace's lungs in a quick burst. A human life or an eternity serving the Guardians as their Oracle. Neither sounded particularly appealing. As an oracle she would be able to help people. But if she lived forever, she would never see Chris again. She bit her bottom lip.

The Guardians were shorthanded. The world was a mess. If Grace had the ability to help, she should do it. Shouldn't she? Wouldn't Chris want her to do that? Didn't she want it, herself?

"I'll do it," Grace agreed. "I'll be the Oracle."

"Good. That solves my dilemma. Thank you. Now. For your secret. In order to end this battle, you must use the Eye of Hera."

"What?" Grace felt a tremor of panic. "No, there must be

some other way."

No matter what her father did or didn't do, he was still her father. She didn't think she could bring herself to use the Eye against him or his followers. She saw what it did to James. She could not bear the idea of doing that to any of the Olympians. To anyone.

"It is the only way," Gaia said in a reassuring voice. "You must trust me on this matter. And now, your gift. You may choose one soul to release from the Underworld."

Chris! Grace almost screamed the name, but her throat closed around the word. Her mind kept going back to that horrible zoo, to those souls stuck in Tartarus.

"Let me ask you," Grace began. "When someone dies, someone good, are they...." She was unable to finish the thought.

"You wonder if your loved ones who have perished are happy?"

Grace nodded.

"For those who pass on, it is paradise," Gaia explained. "Grief, longing, sadness. They are burdens of the living. The dead are at peace."

"Except the souls in Tartarus," Grace whispered.

"That is true, though it is the purpose of Hades to judge the souls. And I trust his judgment. If someone is in Hades, it is because they deserve to be there."

Grace shook her head. "I know. It's just that, I feel bad for him. He did terrible things, but I think he's really sorry. I know what he did, and I know why. It doesn't make what he did right. Isn't there a place where it's enough? Isn't there a time to say, you've served your punishment?"

"You would show mercy on him that wronged you and your loved ones so badly?" Gaia asked, still stroking Grace's hair.

"Yes, I suppose I would. What you said about the power, about the afterlife being paradise. I would like to see him have a chance at life. One mortal life. A chance to get it right, to do things differently."

"Oh, I know who you are speaking of. How do you think

James would feel about freeing the man who betrayed him?"

Grace looked up, meeting Gaia's brilliant blue eyes.

"I think he'd be pissed," Grace admitted. "But it feels right in my heart. I can't worry about what James would want. I can only worry about what feels right to me. I know I could ask for Chris. It's what I want. I want it so much my teeth ache. But I don't think I can be that selfish. Someday I'll be with him again. And until that day comes, maybe I can do some good in the world. I need to earn my place in Elysium, after all."

"That is your choice then? Samael's sentence is to be, let's call it, restructured. His punishment will be one mortal lifetime. After that he will be judged again and, if found worthy, be given his peaceful death. Is that the boon you ask for?"

Grace swallowed. "Yes. Thank you."

"You surprise me, Grace. But mostly you make me proud. Go now and remember what I said. If you want to end this war, you must use the Eye of Hera." Gaia leaned forward and pressed a kiss to Grace's forehead.

It felt like being kissed by sunshine.

"Wait," Grace said. "There's one other thing. My father."

"Yes," Gaia said with a patient smile. "What do you say to one mortal lifetime for him, as well?"

"Yes," Grace agreed.

* * *

IN a blink, Gaia and the cavern were gone.

Once again, Grace stood in Hades' chamber. The book of the Oracles sat closed on his table.

Opening the book, she pressed her hand to its pages, closed her eyes, and focused.

When Grace opened her eyes again, she was holding the orb. It felt awkward and uncomfortable in her hand, as if it didn't belong, like a right-handed person trying to write left-handed.

With a deep breath, she flashed back to the field in Virginia, preparing herself for the impossible task ahead.

CHAPTER 27

Valor is a gift. Those having it never know for sure whether they have it until the test comes. ~ Unknown

GRACE walked into the center of the meadow, the orb held in front of her.

"Stop!" she screamed.

The fighting stopped. Every pair of eyes watched. as she approached where Prometheus and James fought.

"Finally," James said with a huff. "It's about time you showed up." Then he noticed the Orb in her hand and took a wary step back.

Prometheus also stepped back, raising his hands. "Daughter, surely you aren't going to use that on your own father."

Out of the corner of her eye, Grace saw Apollo advancing on her with his golden bow drawn.

"I wouldn't do that, Apollo," Grace cautioned, her gaze fixed on Prometheus. "Stand down now, and you'll walk out of this relatively intact. The same goes for you, Eris."

Eris glared at Grace, but stood still, her hands on her hips.

Apollo lowered the bow, but just a fraction of an inch.

"Grace, please," Prometheus begged, moving toward her with outstretched arms. "Don't do this. This isn't you."

"No, it isn't," Grace replied. "I know it isn't your fault, not entirely. The power corrupted you. Twisted you. My mother loved you once, so I know you must have deserved her love. Once. But this ends now."

"Of course. The fighting is over. You can take over as the queen of the Olympians. We can make the world a better place. Please, give me a second chance."

Grace closed the distance between them and wrapped her arms around her father, hugging him tightly. "Everyone deserves a second chance," she said.

Prometheus slumped, as he exhaled a nervous breath and returned her hug.

"So here's yours," Grace added, touching the orb to the side of his face.

A strange glow began to fill the orb. Prometheus lost his hold on Grace and fell to his knees.

He must have expected pain, but from the look on his face Grace could tell there was none. The Eye only caused pain if the person using it wanted to cause pain.

The Eye itself was not good or evil. It was neutral. A tool.

Grace held his cheek in her free hand, still pressing the orb to his temple with the other. "Prometheus, I absolve you of the power that has destroyed you. The Goddess has agreed to grant you one mortal lifetime." Grace pulled away the orb. "And I give you my forgiveness and my love," she whispered.

Looking down at his hands, Prometheus cried out.

In a flash Gaia stood beside him.

"Come, my dear child. You have a life to live." Gaia smiled and took his hand.

Prometheus looked panicked. Then an expression of peace and contentment softened his features. He glanced back at Grace and smiled. "Thank you."

Grace stepped forward, kissing her father on his now mortal cheek. "Good luck, Dad."

In a flash Prometheus and Gaia were gone.

Grace looked at the orb in her hand. The heaviness was lifting. She could see the ribbons of power it captured leaking through a single, small crack in the glass. Grace squeezed her fingers around it and clenched. The orb shattered, the flash of power disappearing in a quick, bright burst of light. She turned her palm over and the broken remnants of the Eye of Hera fell into the grass.

Apollo dropped his bow. "How did you do that?"

Grace turned her full attention to him. "I will be keeping a very close eye on both of you." She glared at Apollo, and then at Eris.

With wide eyes, they both vanished.

"Was that the Goddess?" Phoenix asked, stepping up to Grace.

Grace nodded. "It's over now. Let's go home."

James moved to her other side. "Where is home for you these days?"

"That's a good question." Grace looked over at James. "Where do Guardians hang out?"

James grabbed her by the arms and spun her to face him. A childish grin brightened his face. "She made you a Guardian?"

Grace shook her head. "No, she made me something else."

CHAPTER 28

Thus have the gods spun the thread for wretched mortals: that they live in grief while they themselves are without cares; for two jars stand on the floor of Zeus of the gifts which he gives, one of evils and another of blessings.
~ Homer

"WHY would she make Grace an Oracle and not a Guardian?" James complained to Michael and Baal. "We're still one short."

"It is not our place to challenge the will of the Goddess," Baal replied, laying down the magazine he was reading. His dark oriental eyes gave a paternal gaze. "Ours is only to follow."

Grace had offered the Guardians her home in Colorado as a base. It was not spacious, but it was better than their usual plan of squatting in empty houses. She kept her old room and moved Michael into Phoenix's. James was relegated to the guestroom, while Baal worked to turn the basement into an apartment.

"Where is Grace?" Michael asked, opening a can of soda.

"She's with Phoenix," James replied. "Apologizing to the Fae on behalf of the Olympians and forging a new treaty."

Michael laughed. "You say that like it's a bad thing."

"No, of course not." James slammed the refrigerator door shut so hard a jar of pickles rattled inside it. "I'm just saying that we're still one Guardian short."

Gaia flashed into the small kitchen and offered her usual dazzling smile. "My wonderful boys, I would never leave you in such turmoil."

Immediately, the three Guardians dropped to one knee and placed their fists at their chests.

"Goddess, how may we serve you?" Michael asked.

"I've brought you a new Guardian," Gaia announced.

CHAPTER 29

*If you want a happy ending, it depends, of course,
on where you stop your story.* ~ Orson Wells

GRACE arrived in her back yard in a huff, her arms folded across her chest.

"What?" she snapped at James. "I was in the middle of a meeting with Phoenix and her council. I'm still trying to smooth out the mess, so this had better be important."

James motioned to the patio chair. "Sit down."

"Uh-oh. This is really bad, isn't it? Did Eros light himself on fire again?"

"No," James said. "But before I tell you what's happened, I wanted to say a few things to you."

Grace froze. "This really is serious. Okay, I'm listening."

James took a deep breath and sat in the chair next to her. "I know about the deal you made with the Goddess."

Grace interrupted him, leaning over to cover his knee with her hands. "Oh, James, I know you're angry. I don't blame you at all. After what Samael did to you, I understand how betrayed you must feel, but I needed to do what I thought was right."

"Wait, what are you talking about?"

She sat up straight. "The deal I made with Gaia. What are you talking about?"

"What was the deal, exactly?"

"She told me that in exchange for becoming the Oracle I could release one soul from The Underworld."

"And you chose Chris?"

"No. I knew Chris was in a better place. Plus, he hated me for making that deal last time. I couldn't do that to him again. So I chose Samael."

"Wait, you chose Samael? What the hell? You let that lunatic free after how hard we worked to capture him in the first place?" James jumped up, knocking the patio chair onto its side. He paced the yard with his hands clasped behind his head.

"Yes and no," Grace tried to explain. "I had his punishment changed. He gets one mortal life. One more chance to do things right."

"Why didn't you choose Chris? I don't get it. I thought you loved him?"

Grace sat back, stunned. "James, I do love him. It hurts every day that I can't be with him. But loving someone is about doing what's best for them, even if it hurts you."

James snorted. "The ironic thing is I wanted to sit you down and yell at you."

"For what?"

He shook his head. "It doesn't matter now. The important thing is that I want you to be happy." He held out his hand. "Follow me into the kitchen."

Grace frowned, but took his hand. "All right."

James slid open the patio door and let Grace enter first.

"Grace, I would like you to meet the new Guardian," James said from behind her as they walked to the kitchen.

As soon as she turned the corner, her world tilted.

Standing there, in her kitchen, was Chris.

Grace wanted to run into his arms, but she was paralyzed. Too terrified to move in case he was a mirage, a trick of the light that would vanish before her eyes.

Crossing the room in two long strides, Chris scooped Grace into his arms. He spun her around as if she weighed nothing and then pressed his lips to hers.

Pulling back, Grace ran her hands along his face, his chest, and his arms. Tears dripped off her chin. "I don't understand. How?"

"The Goddess," Chris replied simply. "She made me a deal. She needed a new Guardian. I knew it was the only way back to you, so I agreed. And Grace, I remember. Everything." He lowered her gently until her feet touched the floor, but kept his arms wrapped around her waist.

"Point of fact," James interrupted. He leaned against the entry wall, watching the reunion with a resigned smile. "He's not Chris, not anymore at least."

James stepped into the kitchen. Flopping into a chair, he dropped his feet on the table and clasped his hands behind his head. "Go ahead. Tell her your new name."

Grace turned back to Chris, her eyebrows raised as she remembered what James once told her about Guardians being renamed when they were chosen.

Chris winced. "Well, yeah. I was given a new name when the Goddess brought me back. But you can still call me Chris."

Grace smiled, knowing that it didn't matter what she called him. A rose by any other name, so to speak. "No, I want to know. What is it?"

Chris sighed, rolling his eyes. "Ethan. My new name is Ethan."

Grace stepped out of his arms and tilted her head this way and that, looking at him from every angle.

"Well, Ethan, I'm Grace," she said, holding out her hand. "Nice to meet you."

Chris snickered, took her hand, and used it to pull her forward, pressing her against him until Grace could not tell where she ended and he began.

He buried his face in her hair. "Are you really okay with this? I don't have wings anymore. I'll be running all over who knows where with this loser." He nodded to where James sat making quiet gagging noises. "I can't live in Faerie anymore. I know how much you love it there."

Grace looked up into his stunning blue eyes. "Well, I will miss the wings, but my home is wherever you are. What else do you want me to say?"

He smiled, and it lit up his whole face. "Say you love me."

"I love you."

EPILOGUE

GRACE sat on the edge of the bathroom counter, scrubbing her teeth until white foam bubbles appeared in the corners of her mouth as Chris walked over. She still could not quite bring herself to call him Ethan.

He leaned over the sink, his face covered in shaving cream. "This part, I could do without," he complained, gliding the razor across his cheek.

Grace spat into the water running in the sink and then wiped her mouth with the back of her hand. "I still can't believe you never had to shave before."

"Fae don't grow facial hair unless they want to. Not being able to control it is really annoying."

"Poor baby." Grace dropped her purple toothbrush in the crowded duck-shaped holder. "Phenomenal cosmic power comes at a steep price I guess."

She slipped off the counter. Grace was still in her comfortable blue pajama shorts and white tank top, despite the lateness of the day. She had been up all night waiting for 'the boys' to get back from their latest mission, a trip to Pakistan to intercept the delivery of some lethal biological weapon. Luckily, the Guardians were able to locate and neutralize it before the local rebel leader could let it lose on the unknowing population.

It was after five o'clock in the morning before they made it back to their humble base of operations in Grace's Colorado house. She would have slept all day long if not for the banging of the construction crew that was working to put an addition on the small abode.

Michael was still using Phoenix's old room, Baal had finished the basement apartment to fit his needs, and James preferred the space the guestroom offered. It was crowded, but homey.

It seemed odd to sit around a humble wooden kitchen table with four divine watchdogs with godlike powers. Yet somehow they were a family, and that felt extremely good.

A sharp knock at the door made Chris turn his head at just the wrong moment, nicking his chin.

"You two almost done in there? I have sand in unspeakable places and I need a shower." James hollered through the closed door. "Now!"

A tiny droplet of blood rolled through the white foam and dripped onto the rug. "Ouch!" Chris winced, examining the cut in the mirror.

Grace opened the medicine cabinet and produced a small pink bandage. They were the ones she used whenever she nicked her legs the same way.

After rinsing his face in the sink, Chris patted it dry and then saw what Grace held. "Pink? Really?"

Grace puckered her lips. "Well, I can't heal you anymore, so this will have to do."

Reluctantly, he lifted his chin and allowed her to apply the tiny plastic strip.

She leaned forward and gave it a peck. "There. All better."

James knocked again. "Seriously. One bathroom, remember?"

Grace sighed, wishing the renovation would move faster. When it was done, there would be a second bathroom, along with a specially designed room where they could spar and not destroy any walls and furniture, like the hole that now decorated the back of the house.

Chris opened the door and with one look James burst out laughing.

"Ethan got a boo-boo?"

Chris growled in that masculine *don't piss me off* way that was part sneer, part low rumble.

Grace pushed him past James and turned just long enough to stick her tongue out at him.

With a snicker, James tossed the white towel over his

shoulder and closed the bathroom door.

Enticed by the smell of exotic spices and meat, Grace walked into the kitchen, where Baal stood over the stove with something cooking on each burner.

"Smells good," Chris said from behind her. "Do I want to ask what it is?"

Baal turned. He wore a long red apron that read: 'I kiss better than I cook'. His black hair was pulled into a tight ponytail at the base of his neck, giving him the illusion of short hair. His high cheekbones were flush from the heat.

"Spiced lamb and vegetables. Grab a plate." Baal motioned to the pantry with the end of a wooden spoon before turning back to the stove.

"You don't have to tell me twice," Grace muttered, sliding around Chris and grabbing two plates. She held one out to Chris, who took it.

Michael finally emerged from the living room.

Grace pointed to him with her fork. "You better get cleaned up. We need to be in Aletheia in two hours."

Michael nodded. He flashed out and then popped back in looking clean and suave in a gray suit with black trim.

"Cheater," Grace mumbled.

They agreed when they all moved in to keep the use of their powers to a minimum when they were not on a mission. Living in the human world meant keeping a low profile as much as possible.

"Practical." Michael the plate Baal had left for him on the counter. After filling it, he took a bite of lamb. "So good," he said through a mouthful.

Baal had extraordinary culinary skills, which was why he got stuck so often with kitchen duty.

"Where did you learn to cook like this?" Grace asked, helping herself to a bite off Chris' plate, as he pretended to poke her hand with his fork.

"The Army," Baal answered. "An army travels on its stomach, you know. Everything else can be miserable, as long as the food is good, morale is high."

Grace raised an eyebrow.

"Not saying your home is miserable. It's quite comfortable, actually. Except for James." Baal leaned close and lowered his voice. "His snoring can be heard throughout the house."

Grace nearly choked on her bite of Lamb.

Chris stood and cleared away his empty plate. "All right. Time to get going. If we're late for Phoenix's wedding, she'll never forgive us."

In a flash, Hermes joined them in the room.

They gave the Olympians the okay for visits to the main parts of the house. Only the bedrooms and bathroom were off limits. They had been respectful about the rules so far, but the moment that changed Grace would get Hephaestus to put a nifty repelling ward on them, like the one he used on his forge.

"Speak for yourself," Hermes said, lowering his dark sunglasses down the bridge of his nose to give Grace a wink.

Grace followed Chris' lead and cleared her plate. "I still can't believe she's getting married."

"That is generally the progression of these things, is it not?" Baal asked, taking his last bite.

"Well, yeah." Grace paused, dropping her hands on her hips. "But it's Phoenix. And Lynx. It's taboo, right? Forbidden?"

Chris stepped up from behind and wrapped his arms around her shoulders. "I suppose that's the beauty of being Queen. You get to make the rules. Or break them."

James entered the kitchen, grabbed a plate, and filled it. Once he was sitting down at the table, he pushed chunks of meat around with his fork. "After what we've all gone through in the last year, can you really blame her for grabbing what she wanted with both hands and refusing to let go?"

The others just at him gaped.

James looked up from his plate. "What?"

"That was surprisingly romantic of you," Grace admitted.

James snorted. "I'm just saying, if there's something I learned in the past year it's that life is unpredictable. Take what you can when you can, because who knows when you'll be facing down hellhounds."

Grace smiled at the shared memory. James was evolving. Who knew?

"All right, I gotta go change," Grace announced, breaking free of Chris.

He stopped her. "Please, allow me."

She didn't have time to ask him what he meant before he snapped his fingers and suddenly her comfortable pajamas were gone, replaced by a long ruby red velvet gown with corset top that defined her *assets* nicely. Her long hair was coiled atop her head in an elaborate fountain of waves. Around her neck was a red choker with a white pearl heart in the center.

He beamed proudly.

Grace narrowed her eyes at him. "Well, nice. But what good are the rules if no one follows them?"

Chris shrugged and gave an unrepentant smile.

A napkin hit her from behind. "I can't believe you just said that," James said with a laugh.

"Point taken," Grace said. "Let's get going. She really will be ticked off if we're late."

Hermes bowed to Grace and then vanished, followed by James, Baal, and Michael.

Chris peeled the bandage from his chin, which luckily had stopped bleeding, and dropped it in the trash. "All better?" he asked, holding his chin in the air.

Grace smiled. "You'll survive."

He took her hand. "Before we go, I wanted to admit something."

Grace frowned. "Okay."

"Well, before…everything, I guess, I went to see my sister. I was going to build a home for us in Aletheia. Not really feasible anymore, I know. Living here with you has been amazing."

Grace's stomach twisted. Did he want to leave? Was he unhappy living with the other Guardians?

"We should make things more official," he said.

The last words barely registered.

"What?" she asked, genuinely confused.

"Well, loathe as I am to admit it, James is right. We have to hold onto each other while we can, because who knows what's going to come at us tomorrow. What I'm saying is, will you marry me?"

Grace froze, as he pulled a small golden band from his pocket and held it out to her.

"Grace Archer, you are my true love, my best friend, and my home. If you give me the chance, I'll spend every moment of the rest of our lives showing you just how much I love you. Will you do me the honor of being my wife?"

Grace stared at the ring, blinking back the tears in her eyes.

She launched herself at him and kissed him passionately, like she would for the rest of their lives.

THE END

About the Author

Sherry D. Ficklin can often be found haunting the racks at her local bookstore with a white hot chocolate in one hand and a stack of books in the other.

A former military brat and now a military wife, she grew up all over the country. She lives in Colorado with her husband, four children, two dogs, and an ever-fluctuating number of chickens and houseguests.

Sherry is the author of *The Gods of Fate* young adult fantasy series, which includes the following titles: FORESIGHT (Book I), SECOND SIGHT (Book II), and HINDSIGHT (Book III).

For more information on Sherry and her books check out her official website at: www.sherryficklin.com.

Made in the USA
Charleston, SC
15 February 2012